The Octopus Under the Bridge

Alice Kinerk

This is a work of fiction. Names, characters, places, and incidents either are the product of the author's imagination or are used fictitiously. Any resemblance to actual persons, living or dead, is entirely coincidental.

Copyright © 2020 by Alice Kinerk

All rights reserved. No part of this book may be reproduced or used in any manner without written permission of the copyright owner except for the use of quotations in a book review. For more information: alicekinerk@yahoo.com

First paperback edition August 2020
First Kindle edition August 2020

Book design by Alice Kinerk
Octopus cover art by Prabha Karan

ISBN: 978-0-578-73242-8

www.alicekinerk.com

For Che

Chapter One: I Am the Octopus	9
Chapter Two: Walking the Plank	28
Chapter Three: No Stopping. No Standing.	38
Chapter Four: Where People Are Provided For	59
Chapter Five: Huckleberries, Cell Phones, and An Old Black Car	85
Chapter Six: Calling Home	96
Chapter Seven: Help	114
Chapter Eight: A Lot Depends on the Wind	126
Chapter Nine: The Gas	137
Chapter Ten: Home Again	148
Chapter Eleven: Through the Eye of the Storm	156
Chapter Twelve: Midnight Monopoly	167
Chapter Thirteen: Do Not Tell Them Your Name	182
Chapter Fourteen: Run!	193
Chapter Fifteen: Flossie Finds a Way	199
Chapter Sixteen: Into the Dumpster	213
Chapter Seventeen: When Gas Catches Fire	225

Chapter One: I Am the Octopus

One day you're an average kid. The next, you're an octopus.

That's what it felt like to me, Jay Everton, right after I turned fourteen.

***

The day before everything changed is an almost perfectly normal, ho-hum day, the first Friday in September. I am in eighth grade. I am an average kid. Average height, average brown hair, average looks, average smarts, average in my ability to throw a ball. And, like I said, about to turn fourteen.

That morning I wake up to Mom shouting at the neighbor's chickens in the backyard. Every morning for the past week, two bantam chickens and a Blue Silkie (the kind with feathered legs like pajama bottoms) have wandered over from where they lived in the neighbor's garage across the street, taken the long way behind our tire swing, slipped into mom's garden and nibbled our arugula.

Every morning she's shaking the broom at them and shouting.

Breakfast (oatmeal, normal) makes its plop and splatter sounds on the woodstove. Dad is hunched over the kitchen table shoveling food into his mouth, late for his job at the community college (also normal). Mom half-watches the stove, half-watches the arugula, and at the same time is replacing the mantle on the propane lantern she and Dad carry from room to room every night after eight when Tacoma's electricity gets shut off.

Laundry steams in a metal washtub beside the couch. A single Monopoly dollar, having escaped the box, is curled up alongside dust bunnies underneath the coffee table. It's been a warm September, warm enough that the windows are still open overnight, and from my spot in the kitchen I can hear Mr. Messerman next door hollering up the stairs at his son Chase (my best friend) to *get up right this instant!*

Everything normal, everything average, everything just as it's expected to be.

There is only one out-of-the-ordinary thing about the day before I became an octopus: I am in love.

The first day of school is the first time I saw her. Washington State History class, first period. Front row, slumped low, wearing a stiff green army jacket, much too big, as if she had arrived at school the right size, then shrunk. Blond hair, straight as straw. Dark eyes, both in color and intent. Arms crossed over a backpack that should have already been in her locker. Nothing moving but her gaze.

She is beautiful. She is a flower, still half-hidden inside a green stem, while the rest of us are mushrooms. Everyone else sees her, too. You can tell by the way they leave three feet of awkward space around her while shrieking their first-day hellos. Safe to say the students of Pierce Middle School don't know what to make of a new kid. Lovely people don't exactly get up and move to soggy old Tacoma every day.

I stand there, caught by boring people telling me about their boring summers, until the bell rings and I am forced to sit.

I am listening while the teacher takes attendance, listening while the teacher selects another girl to help Sarah find her locker, work the combination, and put her bag inside. Needless to say, I hear nothing else that period and very little from the next five classes either. Turns out Sarah is only in my history class and nothing else.

Nothing except my mind. I just can't stop thinking about that girl. I think about Sarah as the teachers read through the same rules and consequences as last year, rattling off all the things we could do wrong and all the things they'd do to us if we did them.

I think about her as I am eating, wondering where in our push-and-shove cafeteria she'd sit down, wondering what she had brought for lunch, or if she's sitting there with nothing to eat, having assumed that the schools in Tacoma still make lunch for the students. (Does any school in the country still make lunch for the students?) I try to spot her in the hallway after the final bell rang, or out front as students came streaming out the front doors and filled up the street.

No luck.

Wednesday night I have a dream that the two of us hold hands in the scotch broom forest. That's what Chase calls the old parking lot around the back of the school. A bunch of weeds and windblown trash and six foot tall scotch broom plants, anything tough enough to grow in the cracks of ancient pavement. Not really a forest, but once you're inside you can't see anything of school except the roof.

That's all it is, holding hands, but it is perfect. Sarah's hand is larger than my sister Flossie's, and doesn't get sweaty like hers gets either. I notice that in the dream.

"This is where kids come to be kids," I say. And when I look up, the forest has turned into a real forest. Tall trees and mossy logs and ferns everywhere. And we walk in, side by side, hand in hand.

Have you ever woken up and wanted to cry because the happiest moment of your life is just a dream?

On Thursday I see Sarah again in first period. I saw nothing else of first period of course, and I don't see her again all day.

Then, that first Friday of grade eight, the day I didn't know would be the last normal one of my life, I'm walking down 6th Avenue with Chase as we have done every day for years and years.

I feel good because this morning I have a list of things to talk to Sarah about. I could ask her about her family. I could ask where she came from, the name of her city, or why she moved. I could ask her what her favorite class is, or how she likes Tacoma, or what she likes to do outside of school. I could ask her if her old school still cooked lunches for the students, and whether they were good. My heart thumps with possibilities.

From a block back, Flossie yells we're walking too fast. She never wants to be close enough to make it look like we're together, but she won't get far enough back that she can't catch up with a few steps running. Problem is, she has to stop and poke at all sorts of things that she has no business poking at.

Today, for example, she is squatting over the broken pipe on Thurston Avenue that's been bubbling up a red-brown goo for the past month and smells like dead rodents.

Flossie's dropping sticks into it.

I cup my hands over my mouth and yell. "Stop being stupid".

"I'm not being stupid. I'm helping fix this pipe. I'm plugging it."

"Don't you know every breath of that stink takes three months off your life?"

Flossie frowns, deciding whether or not to believe me. Then she burrows her nose into her shirt collar and runs.

One day in December last year, Mom quit walking Flossie back and forth to school every day and decided to make me do it instead. That might not sound like a big deal, but it was. It was a big deal for my mom and dad. Because Flossie was kidnapped once, as a baby.

Of course, no one was ever caught. It happened at the old Kmart while mom was talking to the guy there selling vegetables. One minute she was in the stroller taking a nap and the next minute she was gone.

It was a week before we got her back, and only then because they had deposited her with a couple of old people who couldn't explain how a baby girl wound up on their porch rocker or why they'd spent the past week caring for her like she was theirs.

Flossie remembers none of it, of course, and the only thing I remember is riding in an actual car (a police car!) for the one and only time in my life.

Now, nine years later, Mom and Dad still act like there is a bad guy behind every street corner. Here I am a teenager, and other than going to school I can't do more than walk next door to Chase's without one or the other of them coming with me.

They listen to the radio, they hear about a gang of Phoenix beating people up in Seattle or Olympia, and they convince themselves the two of us are next. They complain to each other about how the police never drive their patrol cars around the neighborhood anymore, that there's no security cameras, no 911, no way to stop the Phoenix from taking over. They make a hobby of worrying.

To be honest, up until a couple years ago I got nervous when I heard a car come rumbling up beside us. I had a habit of grabbing onto Mom or Dad's hand and squeezing my eyes shut until the car had passed. It wasn't like I was scared or anything, I just prefer quiet. There is something about the sound of an engine I will never get used to. It's like a beast on the verge of a giant roar, peaceful for now, but always ready to swallow you up.

Anyway, with parents like mine, you have to be very careful about what you tell them. I will *not* be telling them about the creepy black car with the dark windows that puttered along beside us on the way to school yesterday. It's probably some old guy getting nostalgic about his school days.

Old people have no idea how dumb they look all caught up in the past. We have a neighbor who has basically turned his front lawn into a museum for his cars, and spends time every single day with a pair of large scissors, clipping the grass around the tires, as if he might just jump in and drive away any time.

The guy following us yesterday probably thinks kids are too busy staring at their cell phones to notice a car engine, forgetting that cell phones are rare as gasoline.

Rich folks and government have their sat phones, and for all they care the rest of us can get by on smoke signals and carrier pigeons, or so Mom says.

"Did I tell you about the ping-pong table in the scotch broom forest?" Chase says all of a sudden. "Someone must have hidden it there over the summer. It's a good one. Flat and smooth. No peeling. And the balls are good, too! Not one dent. You've got to see them bounce."

I nod goodbye to Flossie at the elementary school, and a few minutes later we're coming around the corner to Pierce. Chase cuts right, ducking around the back of the building toward the scotch broom forest, and I follow.

"I missed this place," I say. The scotch broom grew a lot over the summer. Get big fast so no one can rip you out by the roots. That's evolution. The seeds have popped their shells during the hottest days of the summer, and the left-behind husks cling to the stringy fronds, fuzzy and black as rotten fruit.

"Let's check out the ping-pong table."

It's almost nine. "Not now."

"Yes, now. You haven't wanted to do anything I wanted to do for a week."

For as long as I can remember Chase and I had been friends. And, for as long as I can remember, he had been the one to discover things and show them to me. Chase found the rope swing out by Salmon Beach. Chase found the tuft of grass out back where the neighbor's chickens had been laying eggs, and dragged me along, wanting me to help chuck them at the old post office. Most of the time, if Chase hadn't discovered it, he wasn't interested.

I've already decided not to tell him about Sarah. He'd sabotage it. For a best friend, he's pretty fond of sabotaging things.

In fact, now that I think about it, that's pretty much what friendship is to Chase: Ruin stuff I like, and get me to like stuff he likes.

From inside of the scotch broom there is the sound of arguing, then laughter. A ball hits the table. "You played after school yesterday?" I ask.

"Nope. Too crowded." Chase shakes his head. "I came out here *during* school."

Chase also likes to make things up. "Sure you did. How'd you convince them to let you out of class?"

"Slipped right out the window during first period."

"I'm in that class." I shake my head. "I didn't see you go."

Chase wraps both hands around the thin striped trunk of a scotch broom and shakes it like he's choking someone. Spent husks clatter quietly to the ground. "You didn't see me *not* go."

That's true. I had walked out of first period by myself yesterday, briefly wondering why Chase wasn't there complaining about how the class was boring while the teacher was right there to hear it. The thought hadn't stuck because it had been swallowed up by thoughts of Sarah.

"Getting out is easy." Chase throws an arm around my shoulder like he's my dad. "The hard part is getting back in."

I shake my head, already walking away. "After school."

"Yellow-bellied jellyfish!" Chase yells.

I keep walking. I have things to do, people to see.

A few minutes later, once I am in the same room with Sarah, my heartbeat quickens. I try to think of a question to ask her, but all my interesting questions walked out the moment I walked into the room.

Then the worst happens. There I am, standing three feet from her desk, trying to dig up a question to ask, even just one single interesting question, when she raises her chin from the cavernous army jacket and looks at me.

Right at me, hard.

She even frowns a little, like she can see inside to my hummingbird heart.

"Hi," I say.

"Hi," Sarah says.

Performance over. I take my seat.

The bell rings, Mrs. Markus goes to close the door, and just then Chase comes running in, out of breath, nearly colliding with her. Mrs. Markus is annoyed.

Chase pats me on the head as he slides past.

Mrs. Markus hands out our Washington State History textbooks and tells us to skim through them to get an idea of what we will be learning.

I am always quiet in class, and most kids are going to be pretty quiet on the first few days, getting used to things, but Sarah's hand shoots right up. "I'm interested in the picture on the next-to-last page."

Pages flop as thirty-odd kids turn to the back of the book. There, under the heading *Washington State Today*, is a photo of the two American college students who had gone backpacking overseas years ago and never came back.

Maybe Sarah hadn't heard about them, but the story is legend in our house. The backpackers were important because it was their disappearance that caused our government to send troops into three different countries--Middle East oil producer countries with whom we are not exactly friends--looking for them.

I don't know everything that happened, but a week after troops went in to look, a bomb blew up the White House, the East Coast was evacuated, and that was the end of Before.

Luckily, when the bomb hit, the president happened to be touring his underground bunker.

After that there was no more business relationships with Middle East countries. The only oil used in America comes from America. There's not much oil in America, not like there used to be, and a lot of what we do have is stored in reserves.

Next to the photo is a map of the Middle East showing all the familiar countries: Syria, Iraq, Afghanistan, Iran, alongside the bunched-up neighbor countries with unpronounceable names. The map is covered with dots, bright red like chicken pox.

There's a caption. *Red represents former OPEC nations with whom U.S. oil trade has ended. Washingtonians have demonstrated ingenuity and leadership in adapting to modern ways of life.*

As much as I've heard my parents talk about Brent Andersen and Kaylee Leigh, I've never seen a picture of them before. I didn't realize they were from Seattle, political science students at the University of Washington, same place Mom and Dad met, way back when. It must have been Spring when the photo in the textbook was taken, because behind them are two long rows of cherry trees, frilly pink blossoms giving the picture an eerie cheer.

Brent and Kaylee. Kaylee and Brent. Their names knock around in my head like pebbles in a jar. They look happy. Were they just friends? Were they in love? Either way they did not look like two people about to go missing, create an international conflict, or wind up destroying the nation's oil supply. And no oil, of course, means no cars, no ferry boats to Seattle. No international trade. No oil makes the world smaller, and at the same time, so much more big.

It's weird to think if they were still alive they would be my parents' age.

"The picture you chose interests me, too, Sarah." Mrs. Markus sets her mouth in a frown. "Think about it. These two kids go to the Middle East for the adventure of a lifetime, and what happens but they land right in the hornets' nest."

"They have hornets in the Middle East?" Chase blurts.

Mrs. Markus looked surprised. "No." Then she shook her head. "Yes. I don't know. It's a metaphor."

I watch Chase smirk and look around the room for acknowledgement.

"The point is, it was the actions of these two kids that brought about the beginning of the end. The end of the way things used to be, Before."

"These jerks ruined Before? Can I draw mustaches on them?" Chase holds up his pencil like he's expecting her to say yes.

Mrs. Markus shakes her head, not impatient yet, or just hiding it. "Of course not. They aren't the enemy. They're victims like the rest of us."

Chase flips a couple pages. "Then who can I draw mustaches on?"

"Put the pencil down. You won't find any villains in our Washington State History book. The real bad guys live far away." She holds up the textbook and runs her finger over the middle-east chickenpox. "Here. Greedy heads of state who want all remaining oil for themselves, and don't care what happens to innocent Americans. *They* brought about the end of Before, not us."

Mrs. Markus points to a kid behind me. "Charlie?"

"But there are bad people here too?"

"Yes. There are some people who call themselves Americans, but are doing everything they can to be *Un*-American. The Collectivists terrorize our leaders, bully them out of power. They spew anti-government ideas at anyone desperate enough to listen. As you know, there are a lot of desperate people these days, which means there's a lot of people who will listen."

"No one knows for sure, but it's likely Collectivists who destroyed the Columbia River Dam, so you have them to thank for the fact that the electricity goes off each night." Mrs. Markus pauses like she is deciding whether or not to move on. "They shot a representative from Yakima last winter, remember?"

No one says anything. I rack my brain, wanting to be the only kid in the class who could recall the incident with her. The term *Collectivist* I knew I'd heard Dad say, but it had been so long ago I couldn't remember what he'd said about it.

"And they've threatened to kill many more," Mrs. Markus says.

"Why?" Sarah asks.

"Who knows? I can't explain the thought process of madmen."

Mrs. Markus has a round face. Even though she's at least forty you can still tell what she looked like as a kid. "I would say that the Collectivists believe American capitalism is so messed up we ought to flush it and start something new. And of course they think they've got the best ideas about how to do that."

I am trying to remember what Dad had said about Collectivists. I have a creepy feeling that whatever it was he'd said about them, it was good. I have a feeling Dad *likes* the Collectivists. And the way he'd talked about them, I knew whoever he had been talking to liked them, too.

Right then and there, listening to Mrs. Markus, a memory bubbled to the surface. And right then and there that memory became secret.

Sarah's hand is up again but Mrs. Markus doesn't see it. "What I want you to remember though, is that even the Collectivists are victims. They are wrongheaded, dangerous, and bloodthirsty, but they are victims. No one liked seeing Before end. It scared people and made them sad. Others got mad and wanted action. So, the Collectivists formed. Every villain needs a foe, so the Grand Order of the Phoenix rose up to challenge them. Now we've got warring factions, and everyone is scared."

In the pause before she goes on to give the reading assignment, a faint *douk-douk* sound floats in from the open window. If I didn't already know, I might have thought it was a woodpecker, someone's clacking cart being pushed to a market, maybe a neighbor a block or two away, hammering.

But it isn't any of those sounds. It is the sound of ping-pong balls hitting a table.

I whip around to look at Chase's seat.

Empty.

Friday afternoon I am out of my seat and leaving my last period class before the bell finishes ringing, zipping through the hallway and out the front door. I figure if I take my books home over the weekend I don't have to stop by my locker, and can wait out front until Sarah appears. I am once again filled to the brim with questions to ask, beginning with "How do you like it at Pierce?" I am so quick that I am literally the first student in the whole school out the door. It feels weird to be out there alone. Too quiet. Too calm.

The door opens for one kid, then another, then about fifty kids come out all at once.

"Jay!" Chase yells from the top of the stairs. "Hurry up!"

I drop my bag, rip my boot lace loose, and get started slowly tying it back up again. I figure I can do that a few times and make it look like I'm not just waiting. I keep tying like I didn't hear.

"Jay! Jay Everton! Jellyfish Jay! Are you deaf? Hurry up before someone else starts playing first."

I move on to the other boot. Unlace, tie, unlace.

Chase is beside me now. "You said you'd do it after school."

Just then Sarah appears. I see her in the doorway, then I can't see her as a half-dozen girls push past, then I see her again walking down the steps.

"Not now. I'll come over after dinner."

Chase shakes his head. "Mom needs me to carry water in from the pump on Ninth after dinner. And there's nothing to do at my house. I wanna play ping-pong."

"Monday!" I am already halfway to the street.

"What if I'm not your friend Monday?" Chase calls after me.

I ignore him. Chase also likes to make vague threats. Planting myself in the middle of the street, I look one way as far as I can. Every square foot of the street is filled with kids. I scan the back of a hundred heads, scan for blond hair, a green army jacket. Nothing. I look the other way and it's the same, like a swirl of tiny fishes all swimming together. Swimming away. Too many kids to spot just one.

Back at the stairs, Chase is talking to a sixth grader, pointing toward the back of the school. I watch them trot off happily together toward the scotch broom forest.

I was the first one out the door of the school, and now I am the last kid leaving school. I didn't even get to talk to Sarah, and Chase found someone else to play ping-pong with.

Everybody is moving away from me like I'm a rock and they're the water.

Maybe this is the first sign the plank is about to end.

Not yet, but soon.

Soon I become the octopus.

Chapter Two: Walking the Plank

The next morning, Saturday, it's my birthday. I am fourteen. It doesn't feel much different, as I've been thinking of myself as fourteen for a month, but I am looking forward to the pie Mom baked last night when the house wasn't too hot, and a gift or two.

Saturday's bacon day at our house. In the whole world there isn't anything I like better than waking up Saturday mornings and eating bacon instead of oatmeal. I love the way it smells, the crackle it makes on the stove. I love the sound and the smell and the taste of Saturday morning bacon, and I love knowing it will be a quiet day with nothing to do and nowhere to be. It all adds up to a cozy feeling that all is right in the world.

Mom gets bacon once a month from the farmer's market inside the old Kmart. She pays for it sometimes with dollars, but more often she trades for stuff she's sewn, or writing and editing jobs, once in a while babysitting, while Flossie and I are at school. She gets milk and cheese there too, honey sometimes, chicken and beef, mushrooms, dried beans, berries in summer, and whatever fresh-looking vegetables they have that we don't grow or get from neighbors.

Sometimes, if she needs help carrying, Mom makes me come along, but not Flossie. Flossie's not allowed to go anymore, not after the time she came home with a dozen cheese samples stuffed in her overalls.

Mom gets eggs from the old couple across the street. She says she deserves a discount because of the arugula, but she never asks for one.

This particular morning I wake up and I don't smell bacon, so I guess I must have woken up too early. I close my eyes and let my thoughts drift. They drift to Sarah. *Did you know some of the largest octopus in the world make their home under the Tacoma Narrows Bridge?* I will ask her. I imagine her expression: curious and awestruck. *Neighbors, but part of a different world.*

But then I hear Dad talking in the kitchen. Voices heard through walls sound like bones creaking. All tone, no meaning. I can tell by Dad's tone he's worked up about something.

I don't hear Flossie's voice, so I figure I might as well get up and enjoy the part of the morning without her.

Downstairs, the two of them are sitting at the kitchen table in front of the radio. Dad's staring at it like it's an old TV. It's playing the news. Our radio is always playing the news.

"Morning," I say, standing in the doorway. I make a show of stretching, rolling my neck around and yawning real big, like I haven't been lying in bed thinking about Sarah for the last ten minutes.

Dad snaps the radio off and stands up quickly. "Morning, Jay."

Mom, her back to me at the table, doesn't turn. She gives a sigh, her head sinks and her shoulders heave.

"What happened?"

Dad puts his hand on Mom's neck. He looks at her, then at nothing in particular. "They shot the president."

This brings a groan from Mom. "You could have told him....slowly."

"The doctors are doing everything they can."

I stand braced against the doorway. One way an octopus moves is by attaching its tentacles to solid surfaces and crawling. But even slow movements can exhaust the octopus. Its pulse nearly doubles while crawling. Just standing there, not moving a muscle, sweat prickles my forehead and I feel my heart begin to thump hard. "I thought that would be good news. I thought you hated the president."

"Hated him?" Dad swats at a housefly above Mom's head. "Us? I don't think we ever said we hated him, exactly."

Mom takes a white cloth handkerchief out of her shirt pocket, unfolds it, blows her nose, then pokes it back in her pocket. "Disagreeing with someone is not the same as hating them."

It annoys me when adults twist things around to make it look like they didn't do anything wrong. I happen to have a clear memory of Dad saying someone ought to drag President McAllister out of 1600 Pennsylvania Avenue and force him to spend a week living like everyone else in this country. Mom said she's counting the days until they can vote him out.

"It's especially bad news when you think about the repercussions."

"Huh?"

"Who is going to get blamed for it? Which political groups, I mean. There are a lot of people who are very fervent in their beliefs, very strong beliefs, and we just aren't sure which one the government and the media will choose to point the finger at."

"You mean there will be violence?"

"We don't know that," Mom says.

"There could be," Dad says at the same time.

Dad glances at Mom and begins speaking slowly. "I wish it was as easy as just swearing in the Vice President. But the whole country is ready for a fight. We can't just go on, business as usual. Change is coming." Dad sighs. "Right now we are just trying to listen to the news, gather information so we can be prepared. Read a book for a while so your mother and I can listen to the radio. Which Harry Potter are you on now?"

"Seven. Rereading it."

"Excellent. Go read Harry Potter seven then. We will call you when bacon's ready. Okay?"

"Okay," My eyes linger on the pie on the counter. "But I'm hungry now." It has been cut into eight pieces, but one piece is a little bigger than the others. "Can I have pie?"

Dad looks at Mom, who nods once, sniffling.

"Take it to your room," Dad says.

I spend the next hour or so eating pie, trying to read, but mostly thinking about Sarah. I imagine explaining to her about McAllister, and how you can disagree with someone without hating them. I imagine helping her escape from a gang of pro-president thugs.

Breakfast is normal, for Flossie's sake, and afterward Dad walks her to a friend's house for a play date. I've been on page 223 for ten minutes when there's a knock on my door.

"Come in," I yell, but because I haven't said anything for a while my voice breaks. Mom walks in, followed by Dad, and perches on the side of my bed like a bird. She's not crying anymore, but her eyes are red and she's got that handkerchief again, balled up and barely visible inside her fist.

"How you feel?"

"Great."

Dad looks at my face. "We have another birthday surprise for you."

Mom smooths the handkerchief and folds it into a neat square. "You and Flossie are going to spend some time with Grandma. Start thinking about what to pack. You'll leave first thing tomorrow."

"Grandma Jody? In Meridian? On the Key Peninsula?"

I stare. At Mom first, then at Dad. Mom nods, looking like the least little thing might bring back tears, and Dad is smiling the empty smile people give when they're telling you to make the best of something they know you hate.

"How do you feel about that?"

How do I feel? I feel like someone ripped my arms and legs out of their sockets, left them dangling. I feel like the metronome that controls my heart got knocked all the way up to *allegro*. I feel like I could probably make myself throw up right now without even trying.

But I don't want to talk about how I feel.

I want to talk about how the giant Pacific octopus has nine brains, three hearts, and copper-rich blood, blue as the September sky.

"Tomorrow's Monday. I have school."

He nods. "So you'll get a vacation."

"Are you coming with me? Is Mom?"

"I'll sail over there with you two, but I need to come back as soon as possible. Can't stay." Dad shrugs. "Wish I could. Got work. Got a mortgage to pay."

Just like that I'm furious.

It's the shrug, not the words, that gets at me. The shrug is a lie. Dad's lying even if it isn't with words. It's like he's saying this is no big deal. Like we take off school all the time.

"It's not a vacation," I say, a little too loudly.

Mom rolls her handkerchief into a fat cylinder and drapes it across one knee.

"You said nothing is more important than school. Mom, you told me that a thousand times. Now you're sending me away. In September. *Why?*"

Mom nods. "You're right, Jay. It isn't a vacation. We'll stop by the school tomorrow morning and ask your teachers for the homework you will miss. We'll get a copy of each textbook. That way, when you, Flossie, and Dad are on the boat tomorrow you can make a plan so you don't get behind. You will be expected to read, write in your journal, practice your algebra--"

I thump my palm down on the bed. "You're not answering! *Why* are you sending me away? Is this about the black car? Did Flossie tell you about the black car that's been following us?"

Both Mom and Dad are silent for a moment, staring at me. I don't remember the last time I yelled at my parents, and the moment the words are out I feel separate somehow, just off to one side and back, observing my own behavior. I wish I would have said it differently, but there are no words big enough for how I feel, only volume. The muscles around my eyes are tense.

Dad lets the question hang in the air without answering. "It's not about the black car. We have decided to send you away because we are your parents, and it is the job of all parents to make decisions that they feel are the best for their children." He pauses. "At this time, because of this morning's event, we feel it would be best for you and your sister to spend some time with your grandmother in a place that is safe. It's not forever. Just until things settle down."

When the tears come, they are hot. I try to remember Grandma's house in the woods of the Key Peninsula, but I can't. I keep picturing the house in Flossie's *Storybook Treasury*, the one about the kid who takes a long walk through the woods, all the way outsmarting the evil wolf. She finally gets there, she thinks she's fine and safe, but come to find out

Grandma isn't Grandma at all, just that same evil wolf.

Then he eats her.

I wonder how long it will take to sail there. I wonder if it will be safe to walk to the marina tomorrow.

Dad has some more to say about the trip, about how it will be much more difficult to convince Flossie, how I need to support the plan for my sister's sake, but I'm done listening. I flop down on my back on the bed. I stick Harry Potter seven, still open to page 223, on top of my face, and breathe in the smell of old paper.

Sometimes my head feels like it doesn't belong to me. Like someone else is in there, inserting thoughts and feelings where they think thoughts and feelings ought to go. Only they keep getting it wrong. No matter how long I lie there under the book, I can't relax. For the first time the smell of paper does not relax me. I wonder whether the president is going to die. I can't make myself happy about going to Grandma's. My mind keeps somersaulting, looking for a shred of good news among the bad.

Maybe when I come back I will have something interesting to talk to Sarah about.

Or maybe I will never come back. Maybe I will become an octopus and live the rest of my life underneath the Tacoma Narrows Bridge.

Chapter Three: No Stopping. No Standing.

That night, as soon as dinner is done, Dad stretches and yawns like it's been a long day, jumps up to collect plates and announces early bedtime for everyone. Flossie rolls her head and groans until Mom promises to read her an extra *Storybook Treasury* story.

I can't sleep. I close my eyes and they pop open again. My mind zips around like a squirrel gathering nuts. I stare into my dark bedroom, multiplying days times years to figure out how many nights I have slept in this bed. Five thousand, close as I can figure.

After a while staring at the dark, the shapes of my room--my dresser, my wobbly bookshelf, and my desk too messy for homework--they seem to move toward me. I know it's just my mind, but the harder I stare, the more I see them, lurching toward me like assassins.

I wonder where President McAllister was when he got shot. If he was alone. If there was an electric light on in the room. If he saw the man who did it. What he'd been thinking about the moment the bullet went in.

I wonder if President McAllister is afraid.

Finally, after what seems like a very long time, I fall asleep. I don't remember it happening, but it must have because all of a sudden Mom is seated beside me with her hand on my forehead like she's checking for fever. "Morning, Jay."

I pull on a pair of jean shorts and a red T-shirt and go downstairs. Dad's at the table, staring at the radio again. Mom's at the stove stirring oatmeal. Flossie's still sleeping. When he sees me, Dad smiles, pulls back a chair and pats the seat.

The window is open but last night's heat lingers in the still air. I plop down in the chair and spread my bare arms across the cool wooden tabletop. I rest a cheek against it, too.

...surrounded by doctors and trained medical staff. No one can be sure what the outcome of today's surgery will be, but around the world millions are praying for a speedy recovery. Law enforcement spokesmen offered a statement earlier today urging citizens not to take out their frustrations on....

Dad sets down his teacup. "Ready to sail?"

"I still need to pack."

"I packed for you already," Mom says from the stove.

"When?"

"Early." She sets a bowl of oatmeal in front of me and watches while I pour milk from a glass jug on the table and take a bite. It tastes the same as it always does, like milk and honey and raisins, but at the same time it is completely without flavor, bland, like when I have a cold.

I shovel a spoonful in. Swallow. Repeat.

Flossie plops down at her usual place without a word. Her hair, unbrushed, pokes up in tufts like an underwater plant.

After everyone is dressed and bags are ready and waiting, Mom comes in drying her hands on a dish towel. Her face looks like she's holding back tears again, but this time they stay back. She drops the towel on the newel post beside the stairs, then grabs my arms with both her hands and holds tight. "This is the best decision," she says.

I nod, frowning a little. I want to agree with her, or at least look like I'm not still queasy about the whole thing. She gives me a hug, tighter and longer than usual, and plants a loud kiss on my forehead. She does the same to Flossie. Then she pulls the door open wide. The cool morning air swirls into the warm house.

We walk. Soon the three of us are across the street from the guy with the cars on his lawn, surrounded by the chirps and warbles of morning birds. The morning air had been cool in the house, but out here it feels warm already, the sun a white dot in the blue sky.

And that smell. Faint, familiar, that unmistakable sulfur smell of low tide. Dad's explained it a hundred times. The departing water uncovers some of the algae living within it. The exposure sends tiny particles of that algae, too small to see, airborne, to float at the mercy of the air currents, to glide above all the streets of Tacoma.

Those microscopic particles are just now landing on grass and sidewalks and bushes and roofs, on sidewalks, on Kmart, on Pierce Middle School. Settling into the mossy crevices of old cars that don't run anymore. Whirling up our nostrils.

Dad claims to love low tide smell.

Flossie runs a couple steps and catches up with Dad in front of us. She takes his hand. Swings it. "I'll be back home in time for Katie's birthday party at Salmon Beach next weekend, won't I?"

"I don't know," Dad says.

"But most likely I will, right?"

"Maybe."

"You mean probably?"

"I mean maybe."

Flossie drops Dad's hand and walks for a minute without saying anything. Then, out of nowhere, she stops. Just stops and stands. I walk past, but when I look back her head is down and she is scribbling her fingers across her skull, working her just-brushed hair into a frenzy. She rips off her backpack and throws it to one side, where it catches in a web of blackberry vines and bobs six inches above the pavement for a moment before slipping through. She rolls her head back. Her eyes are squeezed shut tight. Her mouth is a grimace, and her face is red.

Temper tantrum coming.

"Flossie," Dad says in a warning voice.

Flossie ignores him. She stomps one foot against the pavement. Hands still in her hair, eyes still closed, mouth working a silent scream. Then her hands are fists and she's punching either side of her head, again and again.

"Flossie," I try, which is pointless because if it didn't stop her when Dad said it, it isn't going to stop her when I do.

Flossie rises in pitch at the same time she rises in volume. The foot hits the pavement another time, then again, again, again.

Then she's on the sidewalk, on her hands and knees, beating her fists and wailing. I get that frozen in slow-motion sensation like with Sarah the other day, like I suddenly have all the time in the world to think about what to say, but simultaneously I can't think of a single thing other than dumb things like *Stop! Stand up! Be quiet!*

When Flossie pauses for breath Dad comes up behind and tackles her.

I hadn't expected that. Flossie hadn't either. I can see surprise on her face. Full body, football-style tackles aren't Dad's thing. But he throws his arms around her chest, rolls over and all at once she's on top of him, on her back, helpless as a flipped-over turtle. Only she's thrashing around too much for Dad to get a hand over her mouth.

Flossie throws her head back and bellows. "Stop hurting me!

There is movement at the edge of my vision, and I turn to see the neighbor with the cars on his lawn pop up from behind a Jeep and stand there, watching us, giant scissors in his hand.

"You're making a scene," I say in a loud whisper.

"Flossie Marie Everton, pull yourself together!" Dad yells, and, for a moment, Flossie lies still. But then she twists around again, waving one arm straight up like she wants the teacher to call on her. "I'm bleeding! You made my elbow bleed! Why are you hurting me? Stop hurting me! Stop hurting me!

Stop!
Hurting!

Meeeeeeee!"

The neighbor takes three steps across his lawn and stands on the other side of his gate like a fenced-in dog. "Something wrong?"

"No. Nothing," Dad yells, as if you can cover up an obvious lie with words, and adjusts his grip around Flossie.

The neighbor sets down his scissors, crosses his arms, and frowns.

Flossie spots him, too. "Help!" Flossie flops in Dad's arms. "Help! *Kidnapping!*"

And at that, as if a secret password had been spoken, Dad lets go.

Flossie is fast.

She leaps to her feet and sprints off, back the way we came, back toward the house.

A hundred feet ahead of her, at the intersection, taking up most of the street, are seven Phoenix. Seven of them, lined up side-by-side. Their mouths and noses are covered with bandannas, as usual, and they're wearing all black head to toe, as usual. The seven dwarves headed home after a long day in the mines.

For a moment it's like I can see the future. I can see the Phoenix reaching out and snagging my little sister, enveloping her in black cloth and violence, transforming her into someone we will never recognize again.

Now Flossie is approaching them. Twenty feet, fifteen feet, ten. At the last minute she darts to the left, quick as a mouse escaping an owl.

And then she's past them, and is rounding the corner, out of view.

Except for Flossie, no one even moved

I stand close to Dad and talk in my low voice. "You want me to go after her?"

Dad shakes his head.

"You want to go back together? You want to wait for Mom to bring her back?"

Dad pokes at his glasses, there's a pause, and he shakes his head no.

"What then?"

Dad doesn't move his head, but I watch his eyes roll slowly over to the neighbor. His arms are still crossed and he is still frowning, like we are government officials announcing more services being cut. Then, even more slowly, Dad turns to look at the Phoenix still lined up in the middle of the street.

Dad is frozen. He is frozen so long I feel itchy.

She came within ten feet of the Phoenix and they never made a move to grab her. Why? Why do they seem more interested in Dad?

"What then?" I say again. "We can't just stand here." On Sixth Avenue near the old K-mart there is an old street sign that says *No stopping. No standing.* That appears randomly in my head.

Dad starts walking, so I start walking too.

Toward the marina. Away from home.

Away from Flossie's backpack in the blackberry vines. Away from Flossie.

Throughout the rest of the walk to the marina the scene with Flossie hangs over us. I want to ask him about why he didn't go after her, but something keeps me from doing it.

Once we're aboard, Dad pulls the start cord and steers us out to the open water. There are only two times you really need a motor when you are traveling on a boat powered by wind. You need it to get out of your slip at the marina, and you need it to get back in again. Pretty much any other time you are just gliding along, pushed by air.

I can tell from the way he's looking out over the water that Dad's thoughts about Flossie's tantrum have passed. It also seems he is not going to explain why we didn't go after her.

Dad snaps the motor off and holds a finger in the air. "Perfect day," he says. "Wind's just right. Let's see what you can do."

I let the mainsail down and tie it into place, then scramble over the halyard fast as I can, flat on my belly to avoid being knocked around by the boom when the boat starts to tack. The breeze is stronger than yesterday. A sharp gust fills out the sail with a sudden, thunderous clap, and the whole boat shudders. Then I stand at the steering wheel, face to the wind, watching the water break over the bow, two sides cutting into a *V*, like we're the lead bird in a flock flying south.

Dad nods. "You got this."

Behind us, the old Tacoma Narrows Bridge, really a pair of bridges, side-by-side, is a huge blue H. From down here I can see rust holes big enough to crawl inside.

Dad sees me looking. "They put the first bridge up in 1940, just a year or so before the U.S. joined the war. Four months later it collapsed in the wind. National news. Must have been embarrassing. They didn't rebuild for a decade."

We pass two other sailboats, one bigger than ours, one smaller. A sunburned man in a row boat casts a fishing line out to one side. There must be a hundred buoys where crab pots have been laid. The only sounds are wind and birds, the creaking mast, and waves slapping the sides of the boat. Below us, I imagine the giant Pacific octopus strolling in and out of ancient wreckage, nodding hello at trapped crab, changing colors to hide from predator harbor seals.

"Tacoma always had bad luck with transportation. In the 1880s they were thrilled to become the location where the transcontinental railroad would end. They pictured millions of people coming through Tacoma on their way across the country. It seemed destined to be a big, booming city."

"What happened?"

"Cars," Dad wrinkles his nose to slide his glasses back up. "Cars happened. For over a century, they couldn't get people out of their cars and into trains. Trains are un-American."

All along the shore are big spread-out homes that people used to live in Before. We pass one, two, three in a row boarded up, abandoned and looted. The glass in the windows is all smashed out and the enormous holes left behind look like eyes watching us. At the next house all that's left are a half-dozen charred black pillars sticking into the sky.

Tacoma has a fire truck, or so they say. I've never seen it. Chase said he saw it getting washed one time. That makes me think about Chase. Does he realize I'm gone yet? I never got to tell him goodbye.

The next house, a tall, grayish-white, two-story with a wide deck facing the water, hasn't been burnt or boarded up. There are a pair of Adirondack chairs in front of the sliding glass doors. It looks clean and perfect.

I wonder if the people who lived there sat on the deck and watched the neighbor's house burn. I wonder if they felt sorry for the people who lived there, or just hoped it wouldn't spread to them. Did they feel like they deserved to be spared? Did they just feel lucky?

"Now there's something I haven't seen for years." Dad points above the deck where silvery strands, barely visible, form a spider web from beam to beam.

"What is it?"

"Christmas lights. Once upon a time they were used as decoration. At night."

"But it isn't Christmas."

"It's always Christmas when you've got electricity twenty-four hours a day."

"Why? How?"

"I'm not sure. It seems unlikely that the power company could turn the switch for one house at a time. But I do know that a lot of big things go on in this city behind closed doors. It's about who you know." He pokes his glasses. "And how much you've got in your pocket."

We sail south, round the curve toward University Place. After an hour we have passed anything I remember ever seeing before. Dad is talking about how we used to sail out to Grandma's all the time, just him and Mom at first, then just the three of us before Flossie was born. The way he tells it--*She gave you an apple from her orchard. You threw it in the water to see if it would float*--It's like it was just last summer, not eleven years ago when I was four.

He starts talking about Before again. I let his stories whoosh past my face like the wind. Growing up these days, you get used to feeling that you were born after the party ended, that you missed the fun. It's like you showed up with the cleaning crew, ready to sweep and mop. You get used to it, I did at least, so it doesn't make you feel very sad anymore, but you never really *enjoy* hearing about what life was like Before. No kid does.

There's an island off our port side. Nothing special, a small blob of land a slightly lighter shade of green than the land behind it. Dad stands beside me. "That's McNeil Island. One of Washington's last best places. The government owns the whole thing. No trespassing. Once we get closer you'll be able to see the signs on the shore."

"They don't allow visitors?"

"There's a prison on it. There used to be. It's not used anymore. But there's a lot of history on that island." He pauses to wriggle his glasses up. "The Birdman of Alcatraz was sent there once."

"The Birdman of Alcatraz?" I picture a feathered man with wings and a beak. It would be hard to keep a birdman locked up. "Who's that?"

Dad laughs as if he's picturing the birdman, too. "No one really. He loved birds and wrote a book about canaries. But mostly he was just famous for being a prisoner."

"People used to be famous for being prisoners?" I can't imagine what a prisoner could do that people would be interested in, or even hear about, or how.

Dad doesn't answer. Neither one of us says anything for a minute. Then Dad starts talking about Before again. Growing up in Meridian, every so often the police would come around and knock on all the doors, let people know a prisoner had escaped. "They would tell you all about the horrible things he did before he was locked up, how angry and desperate he was. They would leave a photo with his mugshot, and a number to call if you saw him."

"Did you ever see anyone?"

"No. But I worried about it. Sometimes I worried so much I couldn't sleep. I used to worry about stupid things." He shakes his head. "But I guess worrying is just something people need to do."

I let this sink in my head for a minute. *Worrying is something people need to do.* Dad is silent, probably lost in times gone by. I yawn. "You look tired," Dad says. I nod. He stands and takes the wheel and I go downstairs to the cabin to nap.

I wake up to shouts. Someone is shouting at Dad. In my first moment, still half-asleep, I imagine the Birdman of Alcatraz perched on our bow, cawing.

"Identify yourself! We have authority to shoot!" I sit up and draw my knees up to my chest, and tuck my head down, as if that would stop a bullet. I don't know if I am supposed to go upstairs or stay where I am.

"Everton!" Dad yells. "My name is Braydon Everton."

My heart is pounding so hard I see white pulsing behind my closed eyelids.

I take the steps one at a time, clenching the railing to steady myself.

"Hands where we can see them!" Someone shouts as soon as my head is visible. I let go of the railing and hold them up.

"Who's this?" The man is standing on a raft a few feet from our boat. He has a hunting rifle tucked under one arm and it is pointing it at my head. Dad has his back to me. I feel a tiny relief that he didn't ask me anything, because I don't think I could actually bring myself to speak right now, shaking like I am. But then he does. "Who are you?"

Dad, keeping his hands up, turns toward me and manages a small smile. "This is my son Jay Everton."

"Who else is on the ship?"

"No one else. There is little room to hide on our boat."

"If there is, we'll find him," the man says, and just then there is a hollow clank as a second raft comes up from behind and a second man hoists himself aboard.

This man bends down and stares hard at my face. His long ragged beard brushes my shoulder. He's close enough that I can smell sweat and woodsmoke. Finding nothing suspicious in my expression, he claps a big hand on my shoulder and shoves me down. My knees bend willingly, and I sink to the stair while he pushes past into the cabin below.

I am still as a statue while the man checks our boat.

Dad's right. It is small. It is a very small boat compared to some of the others in the marina, and I can count the places to hide on one hand. I hear cabinets being slammed open. Are these some kind of modern-day pirates? *Storybook Treasury* come to life?

I wonder what Flossie would do right now if she was here. Scream? Stomp on the pirate's foot? Try to push the raft away? I wonder what Flossie is doing at home, if she was banished to her room as soon as she appeared back on the front porch.

I wonder about Sarah.

Finally, the second man comes back up from the cabin, gives a brief wave, and the first man lowers the gun. I take a deep breath and let it out. The second man, the one who shoved me down, doesn't say a word, but keeps grunting like he's surprised. He folds his arms and stares at me, grunting three times real quick, *huh-huh-huh,* as he takes me in.

Then the two of them face Dad. About three inches from him, in fact. Both of the men are tall, both are wearing old pants torn at the knee to make shorts. Their arms and legs are thick with muscles. Maybe if a person cuts down enough trees he begins to look like one. "Braydon Everton," the man who talks says. He says each name slowly, then takes a step to the side and looks Dad up and down as if making up his mind about something. "Son of Jody Everton?"

"That's right." Dad nods.

The man smiles. "Braydon Everton," he says again. "Jaden Marr," he jerks a thumb toward his own chest. "We know you. We went to Peninsula High School together. All three of us." He draws a circle in the air to include the other man, who still hasn't said a word other than *Huh.*

I look at Dad.

"Jaden. Of course," Dad says finally, clearing his throat. "I remember. Wow!" He clears his throat again, shakes his head, takes off his glasses and wipes the lenses across his shirt then puts them on again and blinks. "It's been a long time. And, what was it...Eric?" Dad sticks his hand toward the second man.

The grunter just stares. I hadn't noticed earlier, but the two men must be brothers, twins even. They have the same square forehead and the same narrow eyes.

"Eric can't hear you. He lost his hearing."

Dad lowers his hand. "Didn't he join up after graduation?" Dad frowns. "Was it an IED?"

"No. He did, but it didn't work out with the military. What happened was, there's another colony up one bay north. Tend to be real lax about security. Partied too much. A bunch of dumb kids who don't know a thing about the movement. This was a couple years back. Anyway, as far as any of us could piece together afterward, this other group had sent out an open invitation for any and all to join them for Independence Day. You do that, you get all the wrong people. Word spreads. Next thing you know we're fending off a full-on Tacoma invasion, both sides throwing all sorts of makeshift explosives--"

Dad waves both hands. "My kid's here."

Jaden nods. He bends slightly toward me. "There's a war on. That's why we gotta keep patrol. Sorry to give you a scare." Then he straightens up and slaps his rifle. "Not that you were ever in danger. This thing's not even loaded. Jody says if she let me keep the bullets I'd just go and shoot myself in the foot."

He laughs. "She's right." Then Jaden taps Eric's shoulder. He gets up real close so Eric can read his lips in the dim light. "Braydon Everton," he says slow and clear. "From Peninsula."

Eric turns to Dad and studies his face real close like he studied mine. Then all of a sudden he lunges forward and wraps his tree trunk arms around Dad's chest and gives him a hug so big it lifts him, for a moment, to his toes.

I realize that never in my life have I met someone who remembers my dad from high school. No one. Even my mom didn't meet him until their last year of college. For all the talking he does, he doesn't talk about school. He pretty much never talks about the eighteen years he spent growing up with Grandma in Meridian. He doesn't talk about old friends, what he liked to do, or anything at all about his life before he met Mom and had us.

Once he's been released, Dad says that we'd better sail the rest of the way to Grandma's if we want to make it there before dark.

"We were about ready to head in for the night anyway. It's just up here," Jaden says. The two of them climb out of our boat, back onto their rafts and start paddling. I sit guiding the wheel and watch the shoreline slide past. The tops of the trees make a ragged line against the sky like torn paper. We're in a narrow bay. A couple of silhouetted houses barely visible here and there, but mostly just trees.

Forty minutes later we're there.

I turn the wheel hand-over-hand to the right and Dad moves around the boat swiftly, putting away sails. We turn toward a long dock, behind it, obscured by trees, I can just make out what must be Grandma's house. I see the steep triangular shape of the roof and the yellow light of a lantern inside.

When the boat nears the dock, Dad tosses me a rope and yells to tie it up. I wrap the thick rope around a dock cleat, grab my bag and wait while he finishes up. We walk up the wobbly dock. I take my bag in both hands to keep from pitching off the side. Jaden takes the dock in long strides, then watches from the lawn. "Jody know you're coming?"

"I haven't spoken with my mom in almost a decade."

Jaden whistles. "Ought to be quite the reunion."

Jaden and Eric cut off across the lawn to their own house. The glass doors make it easy, when you're close enough, to see inside, and that's how I see Grandma before she sees me. And when I see her--even though I haven't seen her since before I started Kindergarten--something strikes my heart like a mallet on a xylophone. She's short, and round in the waist like a pear. She's got long white hair twisted up in a bun on the top of her head and glasses that I already know are always sliding down, like Dad's.

I can't get over what it feels like seeing her again after so long. It's like there is a hole in my memory, a Grandma-shaped hole, that I've been carrying around so long I didn't even remember it was there. But when I see her, see the way she stands, her pear-shape, her glasses, her hair--she slides perfectly into that hole and fills it up, and suddenly everything just feels right.

Finally, when we are just outside the door, she sees us, too. She looks confused at first and for a second, but all at once she smiles an enormous smile and sweeps open the door. We step inside. I smell the way her house smells—woodsmoke, dust, and bacon grease, and buckets full of very ripe apples—and I remember that, too, remember feeling happy here, and right at that instant I feel just as comfortable as if I was home.

Chapter Four:
Where People Are Provided For

Dad and Grandma stay up later than I do, talking, and the next morning I wake up early and take my time before going downstairs. Sitting cross-legged in front of my bag, I take out each piece of clothing individually and set it on the floor so all of mom's folds stay folded.

Dad and I never stopped by the school and picked up my books and homework like we were going to. I'll talk to Dad about it first thing. That way it looks like I made an effort, even though it's too late to do any good.

Grandma's stairs are very steep, with narrow treads, and a rickety little handrail. In order to descend, you have to make a decision. Turn your torso to the wall and take side steps with a single foot, like an old lady descending a mountain? Or, face front and bow your legs out to either side like a circus clown with giant shoes? I go for the clown walk. It's faster. I can hear conversation in the kitchen, but luckily, the way Grandma's house is set up, no one can see me coming.

"Morning, Jay," Grandma calls brightly when I round the corner. "Sleep okay?"

"Great, thank you." I see Jaden and Eric already seated at Grandma's table. I nod at them and they nod back, mouths full.

"Probably did, too, after what we put him through on the boat," Jaden says, taking a long drink of water. "You were shaking like a leaf in a storm."

I look out the window at the boat bobbing beside the dock, and shrug. "It was okay."

"Just doing our job," Jaden says.

Eric stirs his tea.

"You like bacon?" Grandma calls from the stove.

"Who doesn't?"

"Good answer!" Jaden laughs. "We have it every morning. Hogs raised here by the colony. Butchered and processed here, too."

"Every morning? Every single morning? At home we only have bacon on Sundays. All the other mornings we have oatmeal."

Jaden laughs again. "Cholesterol doesn't exist here."

Grandma shakes her head at him, smiling. "Daily physical exercise washes cholesterol out of the bloodstream. We'll put you to work too, Jay, long as you're with us, don't worry."

I nod, wondering what sort of jobs she has in mind.

Jaden takes a sip of tea, holds the tea ball above the cup and lets it drip, then sets it on the saucer. "Actually oatmeal sounds like a good change once in a while." He looks at Eric, who seems to sense this and looks up. "Oatmeal," Jaden says. "I miss it."

Eric smiles at Jaden first then looks across the room to me, smiles and pats his stomach. Jaden sits up. "City folk have access to fancy imported items we don't come by much anymore. There's some trading we do with other colonies out here on the peninsula, but they don't tend to have things like oatmeal. Meat, fish, fruit and veggies, honey, eggs, milk, potatoes with the dirt still on them. That's the sort of thing they bring to trade." Jaden twists his neck around to look at Jody. "We used to be able to get flour to make bread, but even that dried up a few years ago."

Grandma sighs. "No more flour. But you never know. You traded some huckleberries for that box of avocados last year."

Jaden wipes a drop of spilled tea off the table with his thumb, nodding. "That's right. They were good. Who knows how a box of avocados made it here. The Pacific Northwest is a long way from the avocado fields of southern California."

Grandma sets a glass of water in front of me and I take a long sip. "Dad's still sleeping?" I ask, wiping my sleeve across my mouth.

"He left," Jaden says flatly. "Thought you knew."

I shake my head.

Grandma shakes her head back at me like a mirror. "You didn't know. He left early this morning, maybe three hours ago. He said he had to get back to your mom and sister. I don't know how he did it, got up again so early this morning after we stayed up late talking. It's like I told him, you ought to take it easy tomorrow, give yourself a break. Your father wouldn't hear of it. He said--"

My blood is rushing too fast to bother being polite. "But our boat is still here!" I look again, as if it might take off right now.

"The boat is for you."

"I can't sail!"

"He said you were as good a sailor as he's ever seen, and he's sure you will have no trouble getting yourself back to Tacoma when the time comes."

I shake my head, hard, like a dog after a swim. "But I don't know the way. He knows I don't know the way. I fell asleep on the way here!"

I stand there letting the bad news wash over me.

"How did he get home?"

"Walked," Jaden says.

"All the way up the peninsula? How far is that?"

Grandma shrugs. "There's about thirty miles between your house and ours. A person can walk three, maybe four miles in an hour. He started early. If all goes well, he'll be home by dark. He took plenty of water."

"What do you mean, *if all goes well*"?

Grandma opens her mouth, but Jaden waves his fork, cutting her off. "Figure of speech, that's all. Braydon just needs to keep putting one foot in front of the other. Easiest thing in the world."

The muscles around my eyes feel all pinched up and sore. I want to ask about that word Jaden used last night and again this morning—*colony*. The word makes me think of ants, or bees. Or maybe the Jamestown settlers, trying to make a life here all those years ago before America even began.

But I don't open my mouth because if I do, I am almost certain I will cry.

"I'm sorry he didn't tell you goodbye," Grandma says. "But don't spend all day worrying. It won't do your dad an ounce of good, and there's nothing to worry about anyway."

I wish people would stop telling me there's nothing to worry about. It isn't true.

After their breakfast Jaden and Eric go outside to chop wood.

"Help me with these dishes, Jay," Grandma says. I want to run out the door and keep running all the way up the peninsula until I catch up with Dad. Or I want to jump in the boat and sail it back to Tacoma and be waiting on our front porch when he gets home.

I stand slowly. I feel old. Not grown-up, like on my birthday, but old, like my bones are creaking and my back is aching and I need a nap to get through the day. Slow as a slug I slide into the kitchen. Grandma points next to the sink where she's already washed and rinsed two cups. She hands me a towel. I stuff it inside a cup and pull it out again, then set it in the cabinet next to the others.

Why am I doing this? Aren't I a guest here? When we have a guest Mom rushes around making them tea and snacks and picking up their empty dishes. And it wasn't even a question, the way Grandma said it. Her voice didn't go up at the end. *Help me.* It was an order.

A few minutes later, the front door opens and a woman comes in, kicking the door closed behind her without breaking her stride. In her arms is a wicker basket the size of a Thanksgiving turkey. It's filled to the brim and almost overflowing with little blue-black berries, smaller than peas. Huckleberries.

The farmer's market has them every fall. Mom cooks them into jam.

The woman is wearing a long denim skirt, a button-down denim shirt with the sleeves rolled up, and heavy work boots that look identical to Dad's. She brushes past the kitchen and plops down at the table with a grunt. Her straight blond hair, tied loose, goes all the way down her back. She pulls a handkerchief from her shirt pocket and wipes her face, then stuffs it back in with two fingers. "Well Jody, Summer's not over yet!"

Grandma rinses the teapot, gives it a shake and hands it to me. "Gonna be a hot one?"

"Looks like." She folds her handkerchief then leans forward and peers into the basket of berries, plucking out leaves and green berries and dropping them onto the place mat.

I watch a tiny, pale spider pop up from the basket, rappel down the side and start off across the table. He's going the wrong way--heading away from the door. I have the urge to pick him up and set him straight. But this new woman hasn't noticed me yet, and I don't know if I should wait for Grandma to make introductions or just walk up and stick out my hand.

Then the door opens again.

This time it's a boy. A teenager, like me. Tall, blond curls, square-jawed. Maybe a little older than me. He's wearing a faded old pair of jeans, ripped at both knees, and a flannel shirt that's got rips in it, too.

He notices me right away, gives a quick nod, then drops into a chair and stares openly, as if he doesn't know it's rude. He pulls on his fingers one at a time, each joint separating with a hollow *pop*.

"Who's the newcomer?" he yells, turning his head toward Grandma but still staring at me.

Grandma dries her hands on a towel, looking surprised. "I forgot you hadn't been introduced. Andrew, this is my grandson, Jay. Jay, Andrew." Grandma waves a hand in the woman's direction. "Jay, Elana. Jay is Braydon's son. You've heard me talk about him. He's visiting from Tacoma." She walks back toward the stove. I listen as she cracks eggs in a cup and stirs them.

Andrew smiles. "That your boat?"

"My dad's." I nod. "I'm just here until all the chaos blows over. You know, about the president."

"*If* all the chaos blows over," Elana says.

"Didn't he die already?" Andrew sticks out his chin and gives it a scratch.

"Not yet." There are now five or six spiders crawling in all directions across the table. I wonder if anyone will clear them off before breakfast, or just let them wander.

Andrew frowns. "I was sure he was dead."

"Well, welcome anyway." Elana looks up from the basket of berries long enough to smile at me. "I think country life is a nice break from the city. And you can't beat the weather!" There's the sound of plates sliding over plates in the kitchen.

After the second round of breakfast is eaten and the dishes are all washed and dried and put away, Grandma suggests I help Andrew with his chores. "Now that I think about it, why don't you just tag along with him for the day. Andrew does a lot of different things to help out, and it might give you a good idea of what needs to be done. Then, once you've seen everything there is to do, we can discuss what you like best, what you're good at, and come up with your own list of chores around here."

Andrew jabs the last bit of scrambled egg off his plate with his fork and pops it in his mouth. "Gosh, thanks Jody. A minion of my very own!"

Grandma rolls her eyes, then smiles. "What I was going to say was you two are the same age, fairly close at least, so maybe you will find things in common to talk about. Favorite rock stars, you know, teenager stuff."

Teenagers don't have favorite rock stars anymore. I look at Andrew and wonder if he is thinking the same thing. If he is, he doesn't show it.

"I'm fourteen," I say.

Andrew ignores me, pushes back his chair, tosses open the door and steps outside. He pauses for me to follow, then slides the glass door closed with a bang, and bounds off in the direction of a chicken coop half-hidden in the shade on the far side of the lawn. Seeing Andrew approach, a mob of hens rush forward, flapping toward the gate, *bock-bock-bocking* for breakfast. Grandma had said something about feeding the chickens right away, but once he gets there Andrew screws his mouth to one side and spits on the ground. "Dumb birds. They can wait."

He strides off suddenly with long steps so I have to sort of half-run to catch up. I feel kind of guilty ignoring the chickens, but I figure he's got a reason for it. "So how long have you been living here?"

Andrew looks at me but acts like he didn't hear. Instead, he rips a long stalk of grass out of the ground, lines it up carefully between the sides of his thumbs, and brings it to his mouth. It gives a whistle. An ear-splitting, mournful, warbling whistle, like an injured animal. "All my life."

"You were born here? Are we related?"

Andrew blows another loud whistle. I can stop myself from clapping my hands over my ears but I can't help wincing a little.

"No. I was born in Tacoma. Lived there until I was three or four."

"I'm from Tacoma, too!" I don't understand how Andrew could have lived in Tacoma until three or four but been here all his life. "What part?"

"How should I know?"

I decide to shut up and let him show me around, which is what he wants to do anyway.

We walk along Grandma's curved, sloping driveway for what seems like a quarter mile. Twin strips of gravel are barely visible, separated in the middle by clumps of dandelions and other weeds and bordered by dry yellow grass six feet tall, sucking up whatever moisture is left in the drainage ditch. Here and there I hear a rustling in the grass where some bird or rodent is poking around for food, the *shh* of wind, the caw of crows. Mostly it is quiet.

Just before we reach a line of tall trees, Andrew veers off to the right and follows a narrow dirt path that cuts underneath the boughs. Cresting a hill, he stops and stands with his feet apart and his arms crossed, like Jaden and Eric when they boarded our boat last night.

In front of us, the land is completely covered in huckleberry bushes. Tall, ragged shrubs with tiny football-shaped leaves, dark green and shiny as fingernails.

"We harvested almost two thousand pounds last year." Andrew squints into the sun. "And we're gonna do even more this year."

I am trying to imagine what two thousand pounds of huckleberries looks like. Bigger than a house I bet. Bigger than a mountain? I wonder how many times Elana has filled up that wicker basket. "What do you do with them?"

"Sell them, mostly. Jody makes some into jam. We sell that, too, or trade it."

Andrew reaches for a nearby branch, pinches it between his thumb and fingers, slides the berries neatly into his palm. He gets a good handful, throws his head back and tosses them into his mouth.

Then I try. Partway down, the branch forks, and eight or ten of the berries in my hand slip out between my fingers and disappear into the grass. I'm left with a total of two berries, trapped between my knuckles.

Andrew laughs. But they taste good. Sweet and at the same time sour.

"You want to go crabbing?" Andrew asks.

"Sure." We double back the way we came, down the twisting, grass-covered driveway toward the house.

The chickens, spotting us, cluck impatiently. Maybe it's my imagination, but they seem to cluck louder and stomp up more dust than earlier.

Andrew doesn't notice, or pretends not to. On the other side of the yard a half-dozen wire cages balance in a lopsided stack. Andrew disappears into the house to get bait. When he returns he explains how to pull out the little pocket in each cage and stuff the bait inside. The pockets are made from window screens, old and rusting with jagged wires sticking out.

Andrew holds up the jar he got from inside. There is something dark and oily inside it. "Bait. Once you get a whiff of this you'll understand why crabs go crazy for it." Andrew unscrews the cap and waves the jar under my nose.

Fast as I can I clamp a hand over my face and whip my head away, but it's too late. Whatever he's got in that jar is the most foul smelling stuff in the world. Worse than trash cooking on the street on a hot summer day. Worse than the time a possum died under our porch.

Rotten ocean garbage.

Salty ocean death.

I gag and wheeze and fall backward on the grass in a full-blown coughing fit. My eyes are watering like crazy, and I can't help but think I don't ever want to eat crab again. I don't want to eat anything from the ocean again. Ever.

Andrew laughs, watching me. "The Crabby Special. That's what I call it. Fish guts from whatever Jaden and Eric catch, left to rot in Jody's fridge. Watch this," he says, and sticks two fingers deep into the jar. He scoops out grayish slime, holds it up for a minute—thick and shiny and swirly whitish-gray like pearls--then smears it inside one of the pockets, pulls his fingers back out and wipes them clean on a tuft of grass. He hands the jar to me. "Now you."

    I shake my head. "I'm good."

    Andrew narrows his eyes and stares at me.

    I narrow my eyes and stare right back.

    There is probably nothing in the world I want to do less than stick my fingers in that jar of rotten fish guts. A page out of my algebra book would be just fine. One week with a throbbing toothache would be nothing. I never liked being dirty, but I don't want Andrew thinking I am a thin-skinned city kid, or find another reason to laugh at my expense. And, as Andrew seems to enjoy smearing fish guts, I don't see the point of me having to do it, too.

    I glare. I can out-wait him. I get plenty of practice with Dad.

    "Good," Andrew says, dropping the jar on the grass and jumping to his feet. "Fine. Great. I'll get Jody."

    He disappears toward the house. A wave slaps against the side of the boat like a high-five. I imagine climbing aboard and setting sail. I'd swing by Tacoma and pick up Sarah, then we'd sail south to California. We'd run and laugh and fall in love on the white sand beaches. On every tree there would be avocados, and I would climb the trees and drop the avocados down to Sarah for us to eat. And that's all we'd eat. Never crab.

Years from now people will marvel over how young we were when we found each other, and how true our love must be.

I hear Grandma's glass door slide open again and a hollow thunk as Andrew takes a step onto the porch. There is a mossy old stump and a giant rhododendron between the porch and where I'm sitting, so he can't see me, but he knows I'm out here.

"Jay!" he bellows. "Jody wants you."

I wait a full minute to show I'll go when I'm ready, not when he told me, then I walk slowly, fists balled, scowling.

Brushing past Andrew in the doorway, he doesn't say anything, but once I'm inside he jumps down the porch stairs two at a time and strides across the lawn, whistling.

Grandma's got both hands on the back of one of her dining room chairs. When I force my eyes all the way up to look at her she pulls it out. "Sit."

I sit.

Then she walks away. Not what I was expecting. Walks right out of the room, leaving me there. Grandma has a limp but it's a little one, hard to notice. One knee doesn't bend well so she kind of has to throw her hip up with each step to keep it moving.

I watch her limp out, and then I listen to her in the other room picking things up and setting them down. I can't tell if she's actually taking care of something or just trying to sound busy.

After ten long minutes she comes back into the room and gives me a hard look. Not mean exactly, but not friendly either. Then she goes to the kitchen, pours a glass of water, and sets it in front of me. Then she turns back to the living room.

"I didn't ask for water."

She disappears. Another ten minutes pass. The water's gone when Grandma comes back into the room. This time she pulls back a chair and sits down.

"Are you ready to tell me what happened?"

"I've been ready."

"Andrew asked you to help him and you refused?"

"No." I say. I shake my head. "Okay, yes. But it wasn't important. He was trying to get me to smear bait in the crab pots."

"Baiting crab pots isn't important?"

"No. Yes. It was just something Andrew thought we should do for fun. Andrew's the one you should be mad at. He didn't even feed the chickens like you told him to."

"He's feeding them now." Grandma is calm, her eyes on me. "You know, if a person is planning to eat crab for dinner, smearing a little bait beforehand is pretty much required, wouldn't you say?"

I shrug. In Tacoma, Mom would buy a half-dozen crabs from a man who walked around the neighborhood with live ones sloshing around in a bucket. I wonder if I would have enjoyed it knowing their bellies were filled with stinky particles of rotting fish. I wonder if I will ever enjoy crab again.

Grandma sighs. "Now, I don't know if your dad talked to you about this already or not, so I apologize if it wasn't explained before. But the people who live here--and I mean myself as well as Andrew, Elana, Jaden and Eric, who live in other houses on this property but take meals here and share chores--we have a certain way we do things. We have a philosophy that all things should be shared, food and land and even chores, and we live that philosophy in small and large ways every day. While you are with us you'll do things that way too. Does that make sense?"

I shake my head.

Grandma's eyebrows rise. "It doesn't make sense?"

"No. And it wasn't explained to me. Nothing was! Nobody told me the reason I had to come here. My sister is supposed to be here, too, but one perfectly-timed temper tantrum got her out of it, and Dad said *he* can't come because he has the mortgage to pay, but I know for a fact that bill is due on the first of each month, and here it is the eighth of September and the mortgage is all paid up, so I see no reason at all he couldn't afford to spend at least a few days out here with me--which, I mean, if they had to send me here at all--which I also don't get, because every other kid in my school is just going on like normal and I don't know why everything has to be different--"

When I pause for breath Grandma lays her hands on mine. "It's not about the mortgage, Jay."

I frown at my empty water glass. I can't remember what I was about to say.

"Your father is an important man. He can't just walk away from his responsibilities. You know that." Grandma's voice is quiet. "And the reason nobody dragged Flossie here kicking and screaming, you know that, too. Something awful happened to your family nine years ago, something your parents are never going to get over. That kidnapping was a big deal, Jay, you know that. If we still had TV, the local news would have been all over it. You'll understand once you have kids, but after something like that you don't ever want her out of your sight. To you nine years ago probably feels like an eternity, but to your mom and dad it feels like last week."

I wonder how Grandma can be so sure of all this given that up to last night she's been out of contact with our family for years. "They let me walk her to school."

"They trust you. That means a lot." Grandma squeezes my hands. She turns them over in hers like my palms might reveal something. "You are capable of understanding the complicated parts of the world in a way your sister probably can't yet. And you know what? I'm glad you came here. As soon as I heard the news about the president I started hoping you might come."

I tilt my empty water glass on its edge and watch a single drop roll across the bottom. "But all my friends are still in school. Why did I have to leave?"

Grandma tilts her head. "Your parents decided you needed a different kind of education. You are learning new things here, aren't you?"

I nod.

"In this place, in our way of life, we all help out as we can, and in turn we all get what we need. Do you see anyone desperate for work here? Neighbor stealing from neighbor? Any homeless? Phoenix gangs like in Tacoma?" She doesn't wait for an answer. "Of course not, because where we live people are provided for."

I cross my arms on Grandma's table and sink my head down and rest it there. I exhale on the table then press my face down to feel the warm damp wood on my skin.

"It's like that at home, too. Flossie and I have chores."

"Chores are important. If it is your job to stick your fingers in the crab bait to help catch dinner, then that is what you have to do. That is, if you expect to eat dinner. Understand?"

"Understand."

"Good. Now, back to those crab pots. I have my own work to do."

I walk slowly across the lawn, head down like a wilted flower. Luckily, Andrew is still off in the chicken coop. I kneel down, open my mouth for a deep breath, hold it, and try not to gag as I stuff two fingers in the jar.

Jam. I imagine jam. The fish guts are thick and lumpy, and feel like Mom's blackberry jam. I stick my face into my shoulder and suck another mouthful of air.

Jam, jam, jam, jam, jam.

Andrew trots back across the lawn, grabs two of the pots I've finished and carries them down the dock to one of the rafts. I lay on my stomach on the dock and stick my hands in the cold water of Puget Sound. I rub my hands together, working at the slimy fish guts for a full minute until Andrew unhooks the raft and yells at me to hurry up.

We take turns paddling. When it's my turn, Andrew picks up one of the crab cages and points out how a narrowing tunnel lets the crab crawl right up to the bait, close enough to sniff at or even eat a few particles.

He holds the crab pot up in the sunlight and turns it around slowly in his hands, examining it from different angles. "They don't know until the end that they've been caught," he says. "They think they're safe. They reach the bait and they think *It's my lucky day! All these delicious fish guts and no other crabs here to eat them!* It's not until they turn to leave that they find out they're caught."

I laugh. "Once they know they're caught, do they get mad?"

"Or do they think *Well played, humans.*" Andrew gives a salute.

We move out away from Grandma's house toward the mouth of the bay. On the raft everything looks different. It's hard to believe it was only yesterday I arrived. I don't recognize anything.

The bay widens. To the right of us is a wide grassy outcropping, sticking out into the water sharp as a nose. Andrew says it's a trading location for people up and down the sound. *What people?* I wonder. The few houses I see here aren't ripped apart like the ones we passed in Tacoma, but look dark and abandoned.

We paddle to a place just outside the bay where the currents meet. I can tell because the water is choppier here, and it's windy. Our little raft bobs around and I can't help thinking of Flossie's bathtub toys. Andrew and I scramble around on our hands and knees, tossing the crab pots over. It doesn't take long. I watch the last one disappear, sinking quickly into shadow, a barely visible outline, then gone. A pockmarked old buoy attached to the end of each rope pops up to mark the spot.

Once we're done throwing all the pots the raft steadies a bit. Andrew stands, holding the oar like a cane, squints east, then suddenly plops to his knees on the raft.

"Now we wait."

And so Andrew and I spend the rest of the morning floating aimlessly around the bay waiting for the crab below us. I wonder what time it is and what class period. Pierce Middle School seems to exist in a different world.

"Crab's a bottom feeder." Andrew says after a long time. "Rodents of the sea."

"Gross."

"Jody says it used to cost a lot, Before, to buy them. I never knew why, since they're easy to catch."

"They taste good, maybe."

"No, that can't be it," Andrew says. "Lots of food that tastes good used to be cheap, Before. Eggs, for one, but they're easy to get, too. But stuff you wouldn't expect." He thinks for a minute. "Sugar. Jody says it used to cost less than honey. And sugar doesn't grow here. It makes no sense."

Just the word *sugar* gets my mouth watering. Who knows why. I couldn't even say what sugar looks like. Is it liquid or solid?

I do remember eating a bowl of bright red Jello that had sugar in it once when I was four. I'd been sick, and Mom had been digging through the cabinets for something I could keep down. I remember the Jello because it was delicious--super sweet and fruity, but not like actual fruit. It tasted like a flower. Like something you know you aren't supposed to eat, but is so delicious you can't stop. I also remember loving how the Jello wiggled on my spoon. I loved its color, how it tasted, how it smelled. I had dreams for a long time about bathtubs filled with Jello.

"Have you ever tasted sugar?" I ask.

"Sure. I mean, we used to have sugar all the time, in Tacoma," Andrew says. He is lying on his back on the raft staring up at the sky. All blue, no clouds. And it's getting hot.

I wonder if Andrew has a lot of memories about living in Tacoma, and if it is hard to live so far away, where no one shares your memories and you never get to see the place you used to know. If it was me I would start to feel a little crazy after a while, remembering things that no one else remembers.

"My brother and I used to walk to the gas station by our house. They had a machine with cold drinks that swirled around all day inside a plastic case. My mom always said it was nothing but sugar water." Andrew smiles. "The case had two parts: one blue, one red, with a divider down the middle. They were made with little chips of ice. You could see it right through the plastic. Blue ice and red ice just swirling around all day. Just the sight of it would make anybody thirsty."

"How did you drink it?"

"If you wanted a drink you got a paper cup from the stack. Then you pressed the cup against a plastic lever, and the drink just squirted right into your cup. They gave out the cups and plastic lids and straws for free."

"What was the gas station called?"

"Quick Stop. I remember Patrick yelling up the stairs to our mom, 'Me and Andrew are going to Quick Stop!' She would always tell him to hold my hand and watch out for traffic, even though there wasn't traffic. Walking home, I'd suck on that plastic straw so hard I gave myself a headache."

"You were lucky."

Andrew shrugs.

"So you remember what it was like Before?"

"Yes and no. I remember some things."

"Ever ride in a car?"

He nods. "Lots of times. We had a little round car Mom called the Hatchback. It had special seats that folded forward so me and Patrick could climb into the second row. We used to drive out here to the Key Peninsula a couple times a year, on holidays and in the summer. Set off fireworks, swim, go camping at the state park."

I pick at a loose splinter of wood and flick it overboard. "What was it like?"

Andrew squints. "Riding in a car? Smooth. Like a rock sliding across ice. And fast. You stick your hand out a car window, and the wind will push your fingers back. You stick your head out, and the wind will push air into your mouth faster than you can breathe." He is quiet, remembering.

"But the thing I liked best, on our way back to Tacoma in the Hatchback at night I used to stare out the window at the moon. Something about riding in a car, it makes it look like the moon is following you. It's an illusion. But it made me feel important." He pauses. "Like a king."

One thing I haven't decided is if it would be better to have been born a couple years earlier than I was, so I had a chance to experience Before—sweet, swirling red and blue drinks, smooth-as-ice car rides.

Or if it is better that I was born when I was, so I never experienced those things, and having never experienced them, I will never miss them.

Chapter Five:
Huckleberries, Cell Phones, and An Old Black Car

That night Andrew wants to walk around the rest of Grandma's property.

"It's twenty-five acres altogether, but more than half of that's just woods." Andrew seems to like walking a little bit ahead of me. When I move a little faster to catch up, he just walks faster too, so after a couple tries, I give up and let him go.

"Actually, only ten acres technically belong to Jody. The huckleberry orchard, her house, and the yellow house, that's all hers." He points up the hill where the roof of the house he shares with Jaden and Eric pokes up behind the leaves.

"We do work around the property in exchange for food and rent, anything else we need." Andrew picks a piece of grass, pinches it between his thumbs, and, this time, makes a sharp, strong whistle. "'Course, I'm the only one who's gonna admit all this to you. You ask anyone else around here and they'll just say it belongs to the colony. The Collective. *We share.*" Andrew says this in a singsong voice then shakes his head like it's the stupidest thing he ever heard of.

"And this is the place you've lived since you were three years old?"

Andrew picks up a rock and throws it against a tree. It hits with a plunk and disappears into a fern. "Might have been four. I don't know."

"Don't you ever wonder what the rest of the world looks like?"

"No. I've traveled. I've seen things. Don't *you* wonder what the rest of the world looks like?"

"Sometimes." Waves roll onto a sandy California beach in my mind. "Where have you traveled?"

Andrew draws out a pause, clearly enjoying the attention. "Tacoma, lots of times. Seattle once."

"What for?"

"I went up with a couple friends of mine the other day. We started in Tacoma. They showed me how you can hop on top of the train that runs the coastline by where all those houses with the funky colors are?"

"Salmon Beach? My sister's going to a party there next weekend."

Andrew nods. "That's it, Salmon Beach. The trains slow down just before they enter the tunnel, and you hike up onto this little embankment then wait until the train comes by and you just take a deep breath and just jump." He shoots out one hand into the air.

"How did you get to there? What is Seattle like? Why did you go?"

"The trip to Seattle was incredible. It was life-altering. I recommend it. You know, the best part was how immediately after you jump you plunge into this pitch black tunnel. You barely have a chance to take a breath when all of a sudden the light is gone and all you can think is *Am I still alive?*"

Andrew sees our world in a way I am not used to seeing it. I like listening to him talk about his trips to Tacoma and Seattle. I like it so much I forget Andrew never said *why* he went.

***

Life at Grandma's takes on a routine. First breakfast, then dishes, followed by chores. Lunch when I'm hungry, whatever Grandma needs done next, and so on.

Right away the chickens become my job. Their coos and clucks remind me of the school gym in the morning before school starts, all the kids chatting, running around, waiting for the first bell. I am getting better at giving them their food, letting the pellets spray from my fist like water from a hose, instead of clumps through my fingers like the huckleberries the other day. I love watching them flap and hobble.

Once the chickens are busy pecking away at the ground, I like gathering eggs. I go in with a wire basket hooked over one arm like Mom strolling through the farmer's market. First, I unlatch the coop's wooden door that opens up from the bottom. There is a stick that wedges upright against the ground to prop it up.

Then I check each nest for eggs. There are four small boxes made of wood, turned on their sides and lined with soft dry grass. Most days each nest has three or four eggs in it. They go in the basket. Some are white, some speckled brown, some have a bluish-green color Grandma says is normal for the breed.

Andrew showed me how to use the ground to clean the poop off the shells. You just rub each egg gently in a tuft of grass, then rinse under the outdoor faucet. Sometimes the poop slides right off. Other times it is stuck hard as old paint, and I have to chip it away with my fingernail.

Doesn't bother me a bit. Sticking my hand into fish guts apparently cured me from being grossed out ever again.

What does keep bothering me is Dad. Not knowing what happened after he left here, I mean. Not knowing if he made it home safe. *If all goes well,* Grandma had said. But what was it that might not go well? Not knowing what it is like in Tacoma now, or if Mom and Flossie are safe. What if they *aren't* safe, and there is absolutely nothing in the world I can do to help them?

Which is worse: Not knowing, or finding out bad news?

Bad news, I think at first. But I change my mind. The past few days with the same questions rolling around in my head have been the worst. Not knowing is worse. Not knowing can drive a person crazy.

The next morning after everyone's eaten breakfast and the two of us are alone in the kitchen washing dishes, I take a deep breath, and ask Grandma if she has a phone.

Grandma dunks a plate in the dish tub and turns to look at me. "What on earth do you want with a telephone?" The way she says it, it's like she's imagining I am planning to dress it in doll clothes, or use it for a hammer. "Have you ever even used a telephone before?"

"Sure," I say. Although honestly, the only time I've used a phone is during Dad's emergency drills, where Flossie and I have to practice dialing home. But for practice, we only touch the buttons, we don't press them. The phone stays off the whole time. I have never actually used a phone to make a call. "I want to call Dad."

Grandma shakes her head as if shaking away the idea. "Are you worried about him? Don't. I'm sure he's fine. He's street smart, like I told you. And besides, who would you call? Your folks don't have a phone."

"Yes they do. It's for emergencies only." I try to remember if I've ever heard it ring. I can't think of a single time. I'm not even sure it works.

"He never told me that. Huh."

"So, do you?"

"Do I what?"

"Do you have a phone?"

Grandma turns back around to me, but this time her tone has changed. "It's for emergencies only."

***

The rest of the day I'm in a foul mood. The way I see it, I was sent out here due to events beyond my control, and despite that I've made the best of it. It's not like I haven't tried. I have been all over the property trying. Helping out with anything I was asked to do, doing more than I was asked to do. Dishes, crabs, chickens, huckleberries. I've been helping Grandma set the table, clear the table, wipe it, all because I saw she could use help, so I helped her. I've been polite, letting Andrew and everyone rattle on about Before, and listening too, mostly. I've been doing all the things that Mom and Dad would want me to, like they have the queen's magic mirror and are huddled around it watching me while I'm here.

I do all this—I do it with a smile—then I ask one little favor and the answer's *no*. That's not fair. I make up my mind not to speak again until I have Grandma's phone in my hand.

All the rest of that morning I trudge along beside Andrew, doing chores without a saying a single thing. Andrew doesn't seem surprised. He certainly doesn't ask me what's wrong. If anything, it seems he actually *prefers* me silent, and even starts up whistling while we pick huckleberries.

Andrew carries an old plastic milk crate fitted with a cloth liner to haul the huckleberries home. I've got a wicker basket like Elana's. We each use a large square rake with a handle on one side and long metal tines on the other to scrape the huckleberries off the bush.

The tines are spread just the right distance apart to catch the ripe huckleberries while letting the smaller green one pass through. Leaves, twigs, and stray fir needles mostly slip through too, although not always tiny spiders, as I saw my first day. Our next job will be sorting.

That afternoon, with the late-summer sun high and hot, and drops of sweat beginning to trickle down my forehead, Andrew's non-stop whistling suddenly hits me the wrong way and I break my silence and tell him—not in a mean tone of voice but not in a particularly nice one—to quit it.

"Something bothering you?"

"Yeah, like I said, your whistling is driving me nuts."

"Before that. All afternoon. You've been stomping around, scowling at the huckleberries, not saying a word."

I'm pretty sure of those three things he said, only the last one he said is true. I pull the bottom of my T-shirt up and wipe the sweat off my forehead. "I just miss my family." In my whole life I have never been away from home for more than two days. And that was just to sleep over at Chase's.

Andrew stops whistling. I rake through the rest of the bush, the only sounds the scrape of metal against bush and the rattle of dried-out madrona leaves as an occasional breeze blows in off the bay.

It isn't just that I miss my family. I do miss my family, but really I just miss being at home, being a normal kid in a normal place, living a normal life. I miss my bedroom, especially my bed. I miss my books, even the dusty shelf of my old toys Mom set above the window as a display. I miss Sarah.

I'm onto the next bush when Andrew starts up again. I've heard the tune before. Mrs. Markus played it for us. You could tell it was very old. I don't remember the lyrics except for one line, which I can't forget because it's been puzzling me ever since: *How many roads must a man walk down before you call him a man?*

Fuming, I move too fast through the huckleberry bush and the rake catches where the branches fork apart. I yank it through, hard as I can. There is the clang of metal reverberating.

Andrew stops whistling and squints at me from two bushes away. "Slow down. You'll bend the wires."

"The wires are fine."

"They bend easy. Then they're almost impossible to get straight again."

I miss Mom. My mind lingers on the image of her standing behind Flossie with the hairbrush.

The other morning, the morning Dad and I sailed out here, she sat down at the table and watched me while I shoveled in my oatmeal. At first she didn't say a word but then she started asking me about the black car. *Did it slow down when it got closer to you and Flossie? Did you get a look at who was inside? What did the license plate say?*

Thinking about this conversation gets me mad at Mom. Dad, too. It's impossible to bring up a small thing to my parents without them turning it into a big deal. Why was she asking so many questions about a stupid car? Why was she so worried about it? I am willing to bet that at least half of the kids who walk to school the way I do along sixth have never even noticed that old black car cruising by. The kids who did notice probably didn't bother to mention it.

Dad said people need something to worry about. I guess once you become a parent the thing you worry about is your kid. And some people just need to worry more than others.

But if they are so worried, why send one child away, and keep the other one home? And why was it me they sent away, when Chase and Sarah and probably all the other kids in the whole city of Tacoma were still going to school like normal?

Is there something about *me* in particular that attracts danger?

You don't need to worry, I tell myself, but then another question pops up in my mind: Why haven't I ever used a phone?

Lots of people use phones. I'm not talking about the flat ones with computers inside—those are for government—but the little folding phones that let you dial and receive calls only. A lot of kids my age bring phones like that to school. Their parents buy it for them so if there is an emergency or something they can let them know. Why not me?

I mean, Flossie is too young for a phone probably, she might decide to call up her friends in the middle of the night, invite them over for Monopoly, but I am one of the most responsible kids in my grade, and if they gave me a phone they know I would not waste the minutes yakking. And Dad is always so obsessed with the family's safety. So why?

When we finish with the huckleberries Andrew drops his milk crate on Grandma's table and bounds off toward the dock to jump into the bay, which is pretty much what he does every afternoon. I go and sit for a while outside on the bench beside the chicken coop.

The sun sinks toward the west side of the bay, and the air begins to cool. On the horizon there's clouds, and after ten or twelve minutes sitting on the bench a big puff of air comes whistling up the bay, accompanied by the squeak and groan of tree trunks.

A few minutes later there is the clang of Grandma's front door shutting, and from far away I see Andrew striding toward me. He's whistling again, but in his hand he's got something small and square and gray. He tosses it above his head and catches it with the other hand. He tosses it again, catches it again. When he gets close enough I can make out what it is. A phone.

Chapter Six: Calling Home

"Jody says you want this," Andrew holds the phone out on a flat palm, but when I reach for it he curls his fingers up and pulls it away. "We can't call here." He points up the driveway toward the road. "We walk."

So Andrew and I walk. Not side-by-side, but him a few steps ahead and me a few steps behind, as usual. We climb the driveway to the road. First there is a straightaway for about a mile. The road dips into a little valley then slopes up gently again on the other side and bears left, tracing the north shore of the bay.

At the bottom of the dip there is the bubbling of a brook. The tall stalks of grass have been flattened by animals coming for water.

In front Andrew takes long, fast strides and I am out of breath trying to keep up. "So you never told me what happened to your family. Patrick and your parents? Where are they now?"

Andrew doesn't slow down. "Dead," he says flatly.

"You want to talk about it?"
"No."
"What happened?"
"I don't want to talk about it."

"Okay."

We walk. The trees look ghostly here. No leaves left, branches mostly gone, thick trunks dressed in lacy green gowns. Ivy wraps itself around the trunk and chokes it. Even after the tree dies though, it doesn't fall, because the intertwining ivy vines form a scaffold that keeps it upright. The ivy does a good job of making the forest look beautiful while destroying it tree by tree.

Then, suddenly, Andrew does want to talk about it.

He stops, turns around to face me, hands on his hips and his chin out like a bully. "Okay, you want to know? My brother Patrick disappeared. Kidnapped, same as your sister, the only difference is we never got him back. Here I am, three or four years old, and my brother starting out at the high school. Hadn't been in school a month when one day he just goes and doesn't come back."

"What did you do? I mean, what did your mom do?"

"Nothing. Everything. She did what she could. First, she went to the school. Walked all around the outside of the building banging on doors and windows, trying to get the custodian to let her in. But the place was locked up and deserted. She walked up and down every street in the neighborhood, talking to everyone she saw.

He just didn't come home. The next morning she was back at the school trying to get information from the office secretary, but the only answer she'd give was that he had been marked as present in all of his classes, and they don't track where students go after dismissal."

"So did you ever find out what happened to him?"

"He was in school all day. He never came home that night. That's all I know."

I think about Andrew living with that mystery rolling around in his head all these years. Something like that could drive a person crazy for sure. "And that's when you came to live out here?"

"That's when my mom left. She just took off one morning, left a note saying she'd gone looking for Patrick and would be back when she found him. Our next-door neighbor was an old lady named Kendra, a friend of your family."

"I know Kendra!"

"I know. I just told you I know. She's a friend of your family." Andrew shakes his head. "I'd been alone in the house for days and days when she noticed me in the backyard. Apparently I was eating weeds. She came over, read the note, took me to her house, gave me a bath and cooked some food. Then she shipped me out here to Jody's house on the next ferry. That was before the ferries stopped running."

"So what happened? Did your mom ever find him?"

Andrew shrugs. "Don't know. Never heard."

"You never heard *anything* else about it?"

"Nope," Andrew's pace picks up a little. I'm practically chasing him.

"So you don't *really* know your mom and brother are dead. Really they're just missing, is all."

Andrew stops still in his tracks and takes a moment before he turns to face me. "They're dead," he says quietly.

"Okay."

Then he turns and trots off toward the side of the road.

There is something I just don't get about Patrick's kidnapping. I understand that it would be pretty easy to snatch a tiny baby like Flossie was, but how do you go about taking a teenage boy? How do you grab him between school and home without anyone noticing? Once you've got him, how do you keep him from just walking back home?

Seems like it would require a lot of kidnappers, a lot of planning and a lot of luck.

I keep walking, scanning the ground for broken chunks of asphalt, then kicking them and watching them fly, trying to decide whether Patrick may have somehow been in on his own kidnapping. Then, trying to decide whether thinking that makes me a jerk. I know I should feel sorry for Andrew, but I don't. I just do not.

I feel sorry for *me*.

Andrew is up to his waist in grass, making a lot of noise, snapping twigs and crashing through the bushes on the other side of the road. "Huh," he says loudly.

I turn to look.

Andrew holds up a pair of eyeglasses and walks toward me. It's too dark to make out details at first but when he gets closer my heart starts to go *thud-thud-thud*. Brown tortoiseshell frames, thick lenses, a little tipped to the right like they've been sat on.

Dad's glasses.

I walk slowly then sort of lunge the last five feet and swipe them out of his hand like I'm diving for the goal post in a football game, but Andrew doesn't even try to pull them back.

There it is, etched inside the right arm near the hinge, his initials. *B.E.*

"These are my dad's glasses! Something must have happened! Was my father *killed* here?"

Andrew laughs. Not just a reassuring little chuckle, the kind Mom gave when Flossie swallowed an apple seed and got scared a tree would grow inside her. Andrew tips back his head and guffaws. "Now don't get panicky." He's already walking down the road, apparently not interested in looking for other clues.

"Where are you going!" I shake the glasses at his back. "My father lost his glasses here. This is important! Don't we need to stay?"

"What for?"

"To look for other clues!"

"It's getting dark. We aren't going much farther. Make your call. Ask him yourself how he is."

I get down on my hands and knees and pat the ground where Andrew found the glasses, but he's right, it's getting dark, the grass is tall, and I can't make out anything that looks like it isn't supposed to be there.

"How did you know to look in that spot?" I ask a minute later when I've caught up with him.

"Lowest branch, tallest tree."

"What's that mean?"

"I found them below the lowest branch of the tallest tree." Andrew turns around and points up the road behind us. We've crested the long hill. "Look at the horizon. See how that tree we just passed goes up higher than any of the other trees around it?"

I look. "Okay."

"In fact, it has a higher top than any other tree anywhere?"

"I guess so."

"Well, that makes it a landmark. And it's kind of a rule of the road that when you're out walking if you find something important you leave it by a landmark for those who come back looking for it later. Underneath the lowest branch of the tallest tree. I almost always find something there, when I remember to check."

I don't remember hearing about this lowest branch stuff before, but maybe things are different on the Key Peninsula. "People who take their glasses on and off all the time are always losing them. But my dad never takes his off. And he never loses them."

"It's a mystery." Andrew pauses. "You want to hear what I think? There's a spot back there on the other side of the hill where a little creek goes under the road. You probably missed it. The animals like coming early. Dawn's about six-thirty, so the first light is what, six? If your dad was walking around at that time, I bet he saw some animals at the creek and got startled. Ran up the hill, tripped, stumbled, and then still too dark out to find his glasses afterward in the grass."

"You think?" My dad is not one to get startled by animals, but I keep this to myself.

Andrew nods. "Bear possibly. Cougar. Most likely raccoons. Do they have raccoons in Tacoma? If you get up close to a raccoon it'll screech like a maniac."

"You're probably right," I say. If I pretend to agree he'll stop talking and I can think.

"Some nice person came along later and saw the glasses and put them below the tree. Probably there's nothing else, but remind me, and we'll go back and look in the morning."

So we walk. I turn Dad's glasses over in my hands, squeeze my thumb into the narrow space between the lenses, pinching my thumb until it pulses. Then I take the glasses out, hold them up to my face to look at it closely in the dim light.

It hits me.

They're clean.

The glasses are perfectly clean. Just-washed-and-dried clean. Think about it. If a pair of eyeglasses spent several days and nights lying on the side of the road there would be a thin film of dirt on them. Leaf litter. Spotty residue of evaporated dew. The tiny curving trail of some tiny crawling bug.

But I hold the glasses an inch from my face and squint at them, and they're spotless.

Would Andrew do that? Pretend to find them? Why? And what unfathomable course of events led him to take my dad's glasses in the first place?

Finally Andrew stops walking, flips open the phone, and presses the power button. He picked a funny place to stop. There's no landmarks that I can see, and I wonder how he knows the signal is good. Who does he come here to call? Three merry notes announce the phone is turning on. Andrew pokes a button.

"No new voicemails," he says, snapping it closed and handing it to me. "Hope you remember the number."

Dad makes us practice that, too, starting before we even went to school. *Give me your info*, he says, and Flossie and I rattle it off without thinking. Full names, parents' names, phone number, address. Still, standing here in the middle of the woods it takes a bit for the number to come to me.

Andrew scratches his chin and stares.

I flip open the phone and type in the digits just like we've practiced, pressing down carefully on each button, and checking each digit as it appears on the little screen. When I am finished dialing I just stand there not knowing what to do. Is it calling? I can't tell. There is no way I am going to ask Andrew.

Then I press a green button that says *Send*, and the word *Sending* appears on the little screen. Three dots after the word flash, tracking the progress of my call to the nearest satellite dish. It rings, which makes me jump, and quick as I can I press the phone to my ear.

It rings three times. Then there's Dad's voice. "Hello?"

"It's Jay!" I know you aren't supposed to yell into a telephone, but I can't help it. Even so, he doesn't hear me. There are scratchy noises, a popping sound like static electricity on a dry day, then silence.

"Who is this?"

"Dad, it's me! Jay! Your son!" I'm yelling again.

Dad doesn't say anything. I guess he still can't hear me. I don't know if I should say my name again or stay quiet in case he says something. I can tell he is still on the line because I can hear him clear his throat. I am picturing Mom is right there too, head pressed next to his, listening.

Then, in the background, I hear something else. A low-pitched wail.

It's so long and hollow it could be an alarm of some kind, but it's not. It's Flossie. She doesn't cry much—she whines, complains, decides something isn't fair and harps about it from sunup to sundown—but she doesn't really cry, never has.

I don't know how long I stood there, phone to my ear, in the middle of the woods with Andrew, listening to my little sister cry. I am the witch, watching through a magic mirror. I can see them, but I can't be with them. They don't even know I'm there.

Then there's a click, then silence. I take the phone away from my head. *Call time 19 seconds.* The screen goes blank.

"Satisfied?" Andrew says.

I shake my head. "He couldn't hear me. He never even knew who it was."

Andrew shrugs. "Then it will give your mom and dad something to talk about tonight, won't it?"

"It will give them something to worry about, you mean."

"At least you know he made it home okay."

I shake my head. "I don't know that. He could be hurt. I never got to ask about the glasses. And my sister--"

"What about her?"

"She was crying. I heard her in the background."

Andrew sticks a piece of grass in his mouth like a farmer. "Big deal. Kids cry. Maybe she stubbed a toe."

I shake my head. Andrew doesn't have a younger sister. He doesn't understand. "I'll try again," I say, already poking the numbers.

"No, you won't." Andrew grabs the phone. "Jody said only one call, two minutes or less. She was very clear about that." Andrew snaps the phone shut and tucks it inside the pocket of his flannel shirt. The same flannel shirt he's worn every single day since I got here. I want to tear it off his back.

"I never even got to talk to him."

Andrew has already turned and taken a couple steps toward home. He stops and looks back at me. "That's not true. You talked to him. He talked to you. You just didn't get to talk *with* him."

"What's the difference?"

Andrew lowers his eyelids to half-mast, like he's mourning the loss of my intelligence. "I walked you out here. You made your call. Let's go." Then, without waiting for a response, he turns back and starts off again down the road.

My very first thought, what I want to do more than anything else, is drop to the ground and start screaming like Flossie. I mean, it sounds pretty good right now to just start kicking and yelling and let the whole world know how I'm feeling.

The whole world consisting of Andrew, and whatever birds and bugs and forest animals are spying on us from the trees.

But what good would a temper tantrum do? Would it make him give back the phone? Probably not. Would my parents want me on the ground bawling my head off? No way. Then I imagine Sarah out here in the woods, observing me.

Slowly, I begin walking in the direction of Andrew.

I feel like a duckling following Mama, and I hate it. I hate myself for doing it, but what choice do I have? Without Andrew, I'm lost. I'd be eating weeds like he did all those years ago. There are no street signs, no grid like in Tacoma, no landmarks. I don't even remember which driveway is Grandma's.

I may be able to reason myself out of a temper tantrum, but my angry feelings stick like candle wax on a tablecloth. I focus on Andrew's plaid shoulders, picture myself tackling him from behind, wrestling away the phone and making another call with the sole of my boot pressed firmly against his chest.

It's a cracked and crumbling road that we're walking on, with lots of loose chunks of old pavement everywhere, and I give one of these ankle-breakers a mighty kick, watch it sail far ahead, past Andrew, who pretends not to see it and just keeps walking. I kick a few more. It feels good kicking things. Why?

Andrew and I walk for what must be nearly a mile in silence. He's still ahead, but slowed down a little. I keep a few steps behind.

The woods get dark first. All the different shades of green, normally a colorful mix of foliage, begin to melt, sinking from green to blue, to black. Lighter in the close-up places, darker in the back. The woods get quiet, too. The small breeze of dusk is gone and the air is very still.

Andrew stops walking and waits for me to catch up. "I'm sorry you didn't get to have a conversation with your father," he says when I get close. "Tomorrow Jody will let you try calling again."

I think about that. Now that I've walked all the way out to where the signal is best, could I find the place again without Andrew around? Probably not. Maybe I could just walk around with the phone held up in the air until I saw bars on the screen. That's what people do in Tacoma.

"I will, first thing. Too bad we have to walk so many miles down the road to find a place where we get bars."

"We get bars at Jody's house."

Again I have the urge to run up from behind and tackle him. "Then what did you make me walk all the way out here for?"

"I didn't make you walk here, Jody did. She makes everyone leave the property for calls. House rule. Two miles, at least. Jaden and Elana go a lot farther."

"Why can't we call from home?"

Andrew shakes his head. "I had to walk out here with you, you know, and I didn't even have a call to make."

"Only because you don't have anyone to call. You said it yourself--you've been here your entire life."

"I have people to call," Andrew says. "I make plenty of calls. I call my friends."

"What friends?" I say, shrugging my shoulders and craning my head around at the empty road behind us. I know this isn't a nice thing to say, but I feel like I've stepped off a cliff with my words. There is no going back.

"Friends in other colonies." Andrew gestures vaguely down the road behind me then narrows his eyes. "You know, associates of your family."

"Other *colonies*? What are you, a bumblebee? And you still haven't said why we can't call from Jody's."

Andrew groans. "Do your parents allow you to make calls from your house?"

"No, because our phone is for emergencies only."

"Same with Jody. You ever ask them why?"

"Because if we were talking on it all the time and someone was trying to get through with an emergency call they wouldn't be able to reach us." Even as I say the words they don't sound convincing. No one ever calls our phone.

"Call waiting," Andrew says.

"Do what?" I jog three steps to catch up with him.

"Call waiting. Ever heard of it? It lets another call come through even if you're already using the phone. Try again. Why don't your parents let you use the phone?"

I feel like maybe Andrew knows something about my family that I myself don't know. I don't like that feeling.

"My mom said that back when she was growing up teenagers used to spend all day on their phones, using the computer on it, playing games, sending texts, talking. She said that a phone can take over your free time and that a kid can become addicted to technology to the point that all their other interests in life begin to fall away. And she's told me many times that she would never want--"

Andrew is shaking his head. "Okay, I'll give you a clue. Your father uses the phone for his work."

"At the community college? No, you have that wrong." I'm relieved. Andrew doesn't know so much after all. "He doesn't allow his students to call him at home."

"His *other* work."

"What other work?"

"Seriously? They let you grow up to the age of fourteen never knowing about your dad's other work?"

"What is it?"

Andrew puffs out his chest. "If they didn't tell you then it's not right for me to tell you."

Andrew's boot has a loose lace.

What happens next, well, it's not like I think about it first.

One second I see the loose lace and the next my boot's on it and he's down, flat on his stomach, fuzzy chin and cheek banging against the ground.

"I don't believe you. You're making it up. You don't know anything."

That's all I get out before he yanks his lace free and jumps to his feet. "I know your little sister was kidnapped a few years ago when she was a baby."

"So. Jody told you."

"I know there's been an old black car that's been hanging around while you walk to school in the morning."

Dad must have talked about it to Grandma the night he was here, after I went to sleep. Then Grandma told Andrew. Or more likely, Grandma told Jaden or Elana and Andrew overheard. "What's that matter?"

"They think it has to do with your dad's other work. They think the person driving the car was scouting you two out, waiting for their opportunity. Then...." Andrew sticks out his hand and grabs the air like an eagle grabbing a fish. He leans into me and whispers. "It was the same car they were driving when they kidnapped your little sister."

"It was not! You don't know anything!"

Andrew sticks up his hands in surrender. "Don't believe me? Ask someone. Ask Jody, ask

Elana, ask Jaden. They'll all tell you the same thing. Ask Eric. He'll tell you in sign language."

My face is hot. How is it a deaf man living thirty miles away could know more about my family than I do? Why would Dad keep secrets from me when just the other day he was telling me how grown up I am? And now that I am stuck here how am I ever going to find out the truth?

Andrew cuts off suddenly to the right and begins down a steep driveway practically invisible under the grass.

Right then and there I decide to keep my mouth shut about the glasses. Let Andrew brag all he wants about "finding" them, but I'll keep it to myself about them being too clean.

When the girl in *Storybook Treasury* gets to Grandma's house and sees a wolf, not Grandma, she says "You're a wolf!" So it gobbles her.

But I am smarter than that. I will figure out what it is they aren't telling me. I will put together the clues.

That's one thing I know for sure.

Chapter Seven: Help

That night in bed I keep my eyes closed so I won't see the furniture moving around again. I don't feel tired, not even a little. My mind is wound like a toy car. I have Dad's glasses in my hand, and I lie on my side and tuck them under my chin like Flossie with her stuffed zebra, and think.

It takes a long time, but eventually, shifting around on the cool sheets, sleep sneaks up on me.

I dream I'm lost in Tacoma. I am running from an old man wearing overalls. He has a pitchfork in his hand, it's like a fork for a giant's table, and he keeps popping out from behind buildings and waving it at me. I see a sign that says Seventh Avenue. I know our street, Sixth Avenue, pretty well so I turn there and keep running. But the numbers are going up, not down. I pass signs for Eighth and Ninth. I cut across the block and double back, but next time I look I'm in double digits and still lost.

Then the man's daughter pops out of a doorway in front of me, scowling. I hop over an iron gate, and I'm in the courtyard of an apartment complex. In the center of the courtyard, all blown up and ready, is a hot air balloon. Ridiculous, but that's how things happen in dreams.

I scramble into the basket as fast as I can, sort of somersault into it, then jump up again and the balloon takes off and I float up, up, up. Below me I can see the angry old farmer and his grouchy daughter, side by side. The man waves his pitchfork as if he would have liked to use it on me, while his daughter just stands there and frowns.

Then, for the rest of the dream, I float around above the city of Tacoma, spotting our house and the Kmart and Pierce Middle School. And everyone who I see looks up and sees me too. They wave as if a boy in a hot air balloon is the best thing they've seen all day. Some of them cup their hands around their mouths and yell *Take me with you!* And I shake my head sadly as if I wish I could.

When I wake the sun is coming in through the window onto the bed. I put on a hooded sweatshirt and pull the hood up. I slide my hands around under the sheets for Dad's glasses and slip them into the center pocket of my sweatshirt, where I can keep my hand on them all day without anyone knowing. Then I lace up my boots and do the clown walk down Grandma's stairs.

I wonder who I will be joining for breakfast today. I don't hear voices, but when I round the corner the whole gang is there. Grandma, Andrew, Jaden, Eric and Elana. Andrew has the radio tucked under his arm and is cranking the charger handle.

I don't bother to ask what the big news is this time. I don't even want to know. Despite that fact that it is really just Andrew I'm angry at, I walk past the group at the table without so much as a nod. In the kitchen I pour myself a glass of water. I drink the whole thing in one swallow, feeling the cold water inside me.

There are no chairs left at the table and I don't feel like chatting anyway, so when I finish the water I set my empty glass in the sink and head out to start chores, but Grandma turns around as I pass. "Where are you going, Jay? Stay and eat."

She's already up and carrying over another chair. Everyone sort of half-stands and scoots their chairs over to make room.

Andrew studies me while I sit down. I can't tell what to make of his expression. I give him a long, squinty glare and clench my jaw, ready for whatever comes next. Andrew picks up his fork and jabs the tines into his napkin. "McAllister's not gonna make it."

"They said things were looking up."

"They were." Elana nods at me. "That's what they *were* saying."

Jaden walks around the table setting out tea cups. Everyone gets a saucer then a little round cup. Everyone ignores him, except Elana, who says *thank you* when he gets to her. "Problem is they never found the bullet. The surgeons, I mean. It went in one side and never came out the other. They rooted all around in his abdomen, and when they couldn't find it they decided to sew him up again and just hope it was in a place that wouldn't cause problems."

"But it went right through his stomach, and gangrene grew in its path," Andrew says. "And that'll kill you, slow but sure." I wonder if this is the sort of stuff he spends his time thinking about.

Grandma looks sad. "What gets me is this is something he never would have died from, Before.

"They said he had the best doctors, the best equipment, everything."

"The best they had access to. Much of the medical technology doesn't even exist anymore."

"Not even for the president?"

"Not even for the president."

Andrew points at the radio. "The country's gone nuts. Violence, looting. People are getting killed all over the place. Tacoma, too."

Grandma drops an ancient crocheted pot holder onto the table and sets the cast iron pan on top of it. Then she reaches across the table and holds her hands out for Andrew to give her the radio. He stops cranking and gives it to her. She sets it behind us, on top of the china cabinet. "Be glad we live on the other side of the Sound and we're still allowed outside. Now eat."

But once the radio is off no one can think of anything to say. Forks scrape against plates and teacups clink into saucers. Eric sighs. I wonder how he finds out about news on the radio. Maybe Jaden tells him. Maybe he doesn't want to know.

I put food in my mouth. Chew. Swallow. Repeat. Inside my sweatshirt pocket, I grip Dad's glasses like they might grow legs and run away.

When everyone's finished Elana pushes back her chair and begins collecting plates. Jaden and Eric stand up to help, clearing away the egg pan and the empty tea pot and carrying everything to the kitchen. Eric fills up the dishpan and begins washing dishes.

Andrew is looking at the radio like he wants to turn it on again.

"I called your dad this morning," Grandma says.

"You did? Did you get to talk to him? Could he hear you? Is everyone okay?"

Grandma nods, her expression serious. "We talked. Not for a long time, but enough. Things are not good in Tacoma, Jay. And with the news about the president this morning, it's only going to get worse. All last week, Braydon said, they were trying to go about their normal lives. They went to work, they sent Flossie to school--"

"They sent Flossie to school? By herself? I thought they were worried about that black car."

"They were taking turns walking with her and back. He said he and your mom didn't see the black car anywhere. But yesterday, apparently, Flossie showed up at the house just before lunch time. She'd run all the way home from school." Grandma shakes her head, picturing it. "She said she got a message from the office that her dad was waiting to take her home early. So she went down." Just then, Grandma's cat hops onto her lap. She waits while he settles himself and begins to purr. "But it wasn't your dad. It was a man she didn't recognize. He told her he was a friend of Dad's, that your dad sent him to pick her up. I guess he thought she'd fall for it."

"She didn't fall for it, though, right?"

"She liked the part about getting out of school early. But when they got out to the parking lot she saw that old black car and took off like a light. She ran home so fast they never caught up with her."

"Your sister must be a fast runner," Jaden says.

Elana raises her eyebrows. "Brave."

Andrew looks up. "And lucky."

I remember my dream last night—being chased through the streets of Tacoma—and I think about Flossie living through something like that in real life, and all of a sudden I wish I was home more than ever. "That's why she was crying yesterday."

"She's a child. Her fears are irrational. Your dad said she's afraid she'll be in trouble for running away from school. But still." Grandma nods. "She's stopped sleeping. She refuses to eat."

"She doesn't remember being kidnapped."

Grandma's cat stands up on her lap and stretches, arching his back. "No, I don't think she would. People don't start laying down memories until they learn to talk. Words are the brain's memory tools." She strokes the cat's fur, a mix of white and egg-yolk yellow, with swirly brown and black too, and he settles. "Without language a person lives in an eternal present. No past, no future." My eyes follow her hand moving back and forth. "But she's been told about it, hasn't she? I don't know what your father would do if something like that happened again. You saw what it did to him. He got obsessed with safety and stopped coming out here."

"That's why we stopped coming out here?"

Grandma nods.

Andrew dips his finger in his cup of tea and lets it drip, staring at me.

Inside my sweatshirt I squeeze my thumb into the bridge between the lenses, two tiny slides set back to back. It pinches, then throbs. I count ten heartbeats in my thumb. There's a tennis game taking place in my head. I keep going back and forth. If I ask Grandma the question I want to ask, I might start talking about the glasses, reveal too much. But I have to know.

"It has to do with Dad's other work?"

Grandma tilts her head. "What *other* work?"

"You know," I say. I glance at Andrew, whose eyebrows are up.

For a moment no one says anything. I watch Grandma's gaze move from me to Andrew and settle there. "His other work." She sighs. "Okay. Yes. You're right. But now, for the same reason, he believes she's in danger again. He wants to send her out here now."

"But he can't get her here. He left the sailboat!" Dad wouldn't walk thirty miles with Flossie, would he?

Grandma smiles at me. "He wants you to sail back and get her."

"He wants *me* to?"

Grandma nods.

I stare at the cat on Grandma's lap. He licks a paw and then uses that paw to wipe the top of his head. I wish I was a cat. The thought pops into my head out of nowhere. I wish I was a ten-pound ball of fur with no language to lay down memories. I wish I didn't know that the president is almost dead, that my sister is in danger, that it's my dad's secret job that makes it too dangerous for our family to visit Grandma.

"It's not safe. You know that already. There's no telling what you'll be walking into over there. I had to be convinced myself to let you go." Grandma says.

"But I'm fourteen. Isn't this...." I don't know how to say it. "Isn't this a job for an adult?"

I watch Grandma, Andrew, Jaden and Elana look at each other around the table, like they're discussing something without words.

Elana swallows. "Jay, some of us who live here can never go back to Tacoma again. We'd be arrested before we got out of the marina."

"Arrested for what?"

Elana has soft brown eyes that remind me of a deer. It occurs to me I don't know how she ended up living at Grandma's or anything about what her life was like before coming here. "It's all political."

"Everything we do is to help," Jaden says. "We want what everyone wants."

"Which is?"

"A stronger country," Jaden says. "Life back to the way it was Before."

"Oil's gone." Andrew snorts. "We're never going back to Before."

"Of course," Jaden nods. "Not completely back to Before. We want a self-sufficient country with a way of life different from Before, but sustainable long-term, with the peace and stability we need for a post-oil world."

"Will someone please tell me what everyone here did to break the law?"

There is a pause. Andrew's dimples appear with his smirk.

"They say it was a Collectivist who shot President McAllister." Elana reaches across the table and squeezes my hand. "Beyond that, nobody cares. Guilt by association."

I freeze. I'm not even breathing. The word *Collectivist* drops into my brain and just sits there reverberating like the tines on a huckleberry rake. Elana lets go of my hand. I can hear Mrs. Markus. *I can't explain the thought process of madmen!*

"If Jay doesn't want to go I'm sure Andrew could do it," Jaden says. "The poor kid hasn't left the peninsula in over a decade. They've got nothing on Andrew."

Andrew sits up straight and leans forward. "That could work," he says, nodding.

I shake my head. "Andrew goes to Tacoma all the time."

There is a pause. Then everyone talks at once.

"He said that?"

"Really, Andrew? Since when? How and why?"

"For what reason?"

Andrew takes his finger out of his tea, sticks it in his mouth and sucks on it. His finger comes back out again with a *pop*. "I didn't say that."

His words feel loud. Andrew's expression is like the expression on Flossie's doll. Just happy enough to feel happy when you do, just sad enough to empathize.

"You did! You told me you go to Tacoma all the time and you hop a train there and ride it to Seattle with your friends. You *know* you said that. You're lying."

"Not true. You just want attention."

"Enough." Grandma says. "Jay, Andrew will not be going to Tacoma for you. In fact, Andrew will not be going anywhere. When we're done here, Andrew is going to stay and have a chat with me. I've got a few questions for him."

"I think we've all got a few questions for him," Jaden says.

Grandma reaches across the table and takes away Andrew's teacup. "And you're too old to be sticking your finger in your drink."

"Jay, what do you think about going back to Tacoma?" Elana says to me.

Everyone stops what they are doing and turns to look at me. I can think of plenty of reasons to say no. I don't know the way. I don't know how to sail. Not really, not on my own. It's dangerous in Tacoma.

It's against the law to walk down the street. No one is supposed to leave their homes.

But then I think about the sound of Flossie on the phone yesterday. I think about Dad's other work, and the questions I need him to answer. The word *Collectivist* dangles in my mind like a mobile above a baby's crib. I think about seeing Mom again, sleeping in my bed again, maybe running into Sarah, maybe getting the opportunity to save her.

I take a deep breath and let it out.

Even as I open my mouth to respond I haven't made up my mind.

Everyone is waiting.

"I'll go."

Chapter Eight:
A Lot Depends on the Wind

  Later, after I finish feeding the chickens, I help Grandma boil eggs. She shows me how to dip the ladle into the boiling water and scoop out an egg, drain off the water and spin the egg on the counter. If it spins fast it's done.

  While I spin eggs Grandma goes outside to the porch to interrogate Andrew. I can't hear anything through the glass doors. Afterward he slinks off toward the orchard.

  Elana skips huckleberries to pick carrots, green beans and apples for my trip. She and Grandma pack the food into a faded plastic cooler then haul it side-by-side out to the sailboat and hoist it aboard. Elana makes a second trip carrying a large canteen filled with drinking water. She uses a thin rope to tie the jug inside a cabinet.

  Grandma takes a long time rooting around for other things she thinks I'll need.

  Around mid-morning Jaden slides open the glass door and holds up something small and round with a glass face, a couple of wobbly hands inside, like a watch without a band. "I found this on your boat. You pretty good with a compass?"

I shake my head. I've never used one before.

"That's what I figured."

I drop the compass into my pocket where it clinks against Dad's glasses. Jaden waits while I lace up my boots and the two of us hike up the hill to the treeline, passing Andrew sitting cross-legged beside the smoker because Grandma gave him a salmon to smoke, even though there is nothing to do while it's smoking except turn it every hour or so. Andrew works a stick into the dry ground, ignoring us.

From outside, Grandma's woods look solid with undergrowth, too thick to walk through. Wherever there was an inch of space some plant has stuck roots down and claimed it. Salal bushes are everywhere, their squishy, bland berries laid out in a row like keys on a piano. Scotch broom does look like brooms, raggedy old green brooms poked into the ground business end up. Their fuzzy seed pods remind me of the scotch broom forest.

Blackberry vines climb high. Stalks of grass wave a foot above my head. A paradise for green things.

When we get to the place where the fir trees and the field meet, Jaden pushes back a long huckleberry branch and I slip under, into the woods. I have to cover my face and shove through the first bush, but then, under the cover of the tall cedars and fir trees, it's like we've entered another world.

The air is cooler, filled with an odor of dirt and decomposition, the way our basement smells back in Tacoma. The ground is bare, carpeted with fir needles, studded here and there with enormous tree trunks. Untrod dirt makes the ground soft as a mattress. Ahead of us, ferns clump around a fallen tree like tiny men who just took down a giant.

From some invisible perch above, a song bird trills. I look up but it is invisible. "Are these trees old-growth?"

"Second growth at least. More likely third or fourth." Jaden points to a clump of shiny green leaves to our left. "The stumps like to hide under huckleberry bushes. There was a time when the entire Key Peninsula was logged, north to south. There was barely a tree left anywhere. Only a few oddball ones growing in places no one could reach. Of course, that was Before."

"The world was crazy Before."

Jaden turns to nod at me. He smiles, a small smile, mostly flat with just a little curve on the edges. "That might be true. But, over time, they would start to notice what wasn't going well and sometimes, if they could get everyone to agree, they made changes, and things got less crazy."

"So how'd they do it?"

"Short answer? They never did. TV and movies with interesting characters from different backgrounds helped somewhat, for a while. But toward the end of Before, with the economy collapsing and everyone looking for someone to blame, a lot of people took it out on people who moved here from other countries. That wasn't fair. They were victims too."

"People are always looking for someone to blame." I take the compass out of my pocket and hold it up. It looks like a tiny clock, but the two wobbly hands always point in opposite directions. And instead of numbers, it has letters.

"Ready to try that thing out?" Jaden talks about what the letters mean and how to hold it flat and line up the wobbly hand with the fixed one so they point the same direction. Then, for an hour or so, Jaden and I trample around in the woods, practicing with the compass.

He unzips a pocket and pulls out an apple. I close my eyes while he hides it. When he's done he tells me which direction it's in and how many steps to take. Then I have to line up the compass and find it.

The first one is hard. Jaden says fifteen steps northeast, but the compass jiggles and what I thought was right lands me on top of the fallen tree. I get down on my hands and knees and paw through ferns and half-rotted wood until Jaden gets me on the right course again.

But after that it gets easier. I learn how to hold my arm just right to keep the arrow still. Pretty soon I am finding the apple in two minutes, down from ten.

After I have found the apple seven times, Jaden says time to call it a day, so we duck back out through the huckleberry and walk side by side down the sunny driveway. There is a greenish-brown smear on my jeans from climbing over mossy logs and lying flat on my belly on the ground. I take a big bite of the apple and chew, feeling happy. Or something close to happy.

"You remind me of your dad when we were in school," Jaden says while we walk back down the driveway toward Grandma's.

"What was he like?"

"Like you. Always asking questions. He always wanted to know *why*. The teacher would explain something, and he would raise his hand and ask questions nobody else had thought to ask. We had lots of classes together at your age. But by the time we got to high school, I didn't see him much anymore. They put your dad in the advanced classes, while me and Eric were stuck with the kids who didn't ask why."

Talking about my dad makes me smile. "He's changed. He likes to explain now. He teaches science at Tacoma Community College."

Jaden smiles. "He sees the big picture."

"What do you mean?"

Jaden pauses. "Well, like you were saying about people coming back from war and deciding to fight for equal rights at home. More recently, they started to see environmental problems, that oil would eventually run out and we wouldn't be able to keep things going the way they were forever. Most people ignored it, because that was easier. Some believed the small changes our government supported would eventually have us using a new energy source. They bought cars that used less gas and installed solar panels on their roof, they voted for leaders who talked about those issues.

"Your dad…" Jaden starts off, and it sounds like he is about to say more, but then six, seven, eight seconds go by and he doesn't say anything else. Why not?

"What about him?"

"Your dad could tell that Before was coming to an end. That's what I admire about your dad. He has foresight."

"And that has something to do with his other work?"

Jaden is silent.

"I already know. Andrew told me."

"That *is* his other work. Helping people who see things the same way he does. Helping us, for one, and other groups like us."

I can think of a few more questions I would like to ask, but by that time we're back at Grandma's. She's standing outside, by the pond, waiting for Jaden and me.

"There you are," she says when we get close enough. "Jay, I have something you need to look at." I follow her inside. The house looks dark after so much sunshine. I sit down to wait as she clears the table. Napkins, a teacup, six placemats and a tiny vase filled with tiny blue flowers Elana gathered.

Grandma plods off to another room and returns carrying an old map. Carefully, handling only the edges, she unfolds the old map and smooths it gently with her hands so it lays flat.

For a minute she stares at it without saying anything. There's no roads and streets marked like on a regular map, but it shows the whole sound, from the state capitol Olympia in the south all the way north to where British Columbia juts in above the Strait of Juan de Fuca. To the left there's the upside down triangle of the Olympics, the piece of land that gives America its square left shoulder. In the north the water is wide open toward the ocean. In the middle is a messy convergence of islands, peninsulas, and inlets. Puget Sound.

Grandma drops her finger onto a piece of land on the bottom end of the sound. "Here's where we are." I lean in to see what she's looking at. The Key Peninsula points south, thinner at the top and bulges a little toward the bottom toward Olympia, like a hand giving the state capitol a high-five.

"This is our bay." On the lower right side of the Key Peninsula there is a V-shaped opening.

Grandma's finger slides a few inches to the southeast. "This is Anderson Island." Her finger moves north. "This is McNeil. What you need to do is sail between the two."

"McNeil is different. They still have cameras left over from its days as a federal penitentiary. Who knows if they're still working. The land still belongs to the government, so assume they are."

"Dad said when he lived here there used to be prisoner escapes sometimes and the police would come around knocking on doors and telling everyone to look out."

Grandma's eyes move from one side to the other as if she is seeing something from long ago. "I forgot about that. It stopped happening when they figured out they only had to convince the prisoners that the water around the island was freezing cold, and if they tried to swim they'd be popsicles."

"Was it?"

"It was the ocean. Cold in the winter, a little warmer in the summer. Wouldn't kill most people to swim it most days." She looks down at the map. "Your best bet is to cling to the north side of Anderson. Keep as close as you can. Let them think you're a carefree island kid chasing wind around the neighborhood. Keep smiling, in case they're looking at you through binoculars. Then, when Anderson is behind you, pick up all the speed you can and point due east toward Steilacoom."

"Steilacoom," I say, spotting it just then on the map and jabbing it with my finger. "It's below Tacoma."

"That's right." Grandma's cat weaves between her feet. "You may see a train on the tracks as you sail in, but I doubt it. It used to be a regular thing to hear the train whistle. Nowadays not so much."

I nod. Then Grandma makes me repeat her directions word-for-word.

"When you get close to land, veer left. A third piece of land, Fox Island, will be on the left by then. You won't be able to see the Narrows Bridge for a while, but you will eventually. First you'll see Chambers Bay Golf Course."

"It's not a golf course anymore."

"I figured it wouldn't be. They're using it for crops?"

"No. It's a homeless camp. It's called 'Tent City.' It had been as long as I could remember.

"Huh." She shakes her head. "They held the U.S. Open there once." Her finger runs up the coast toward the bridge, the place where Tacoma and the peninsula come closest. "The marina you use is south of here, right?"

"Right. Day Island." I point to a scrap of land that clings to the left side of Tacoma like a hangnail.

"When you get there, pull into your regular slip. Even if it isn't the first empty spot or easiest one to get to, use the one you are supposed to. Take your time tying up. Stay calm. While you're out in public there, and walking home too, act like it is just any other regular day. Don't look scared."

"If anyone asks where I'm coming from, what should I tell them?"

"The best case scenario is that no one's around at all. You heard the recommendation."

"But if they are?"

Grandma is quiet for a minute. "If someone asks where you are coming from, tell them you've been camping with your church group."

"I've never been to church, except for funerals."

"Doesn't matter. Tell them you just got back from the Episcopalian camp. I remember they have some property on Anderson."

"Episcopalian." The word feels like a marble in my mouth.

"That's right." Grandma nods. "Then stop talking. Don't say anything else. Most people, when they lie, they add too many details."

"I should act a little shy?"

"Act like you are just now sensing something's not right. And if they ask whether you've heard about the president, tell them you haven't. Ask about it. People like to tell people bad news."

I let my gaze settle on the map. "Southeast past Anderson, then north along the train tracks until I reach the marina. It doesn't look that far."

"Looks can be deceiving, Jay." Grandma turns away to turn off the teapot that's started whistling. "And a lot depends on the wind."

I think about the moment I open my own front door and how it will feel to see my family again. Dad will hug me so hard my ribs almost break. Flossie will toss her stuffed zebra in the air like a graduation cap. Mom will cry.

But I don't like what Grandma said, that a lot depends on the wind.

In the whole entire Earth is there anything less dependable than the wind?

Chapter Nine: The Gas

The next morning, as soon as my eyes open I stand up and walk over to the window to see what the weather's like for sailing. At first there's nothing. Then a big whoosh of wind sets the alder leaves shivering, sparkling in the sun, and I get a good feeling in my chest, happy and full, like the wind outside has puffed me up too.

Everything was packed and ready before I went to bed last night, so there isn't much to do today except eat breakfast and say goodbye. Eric and Jaden are in the yard hauling off a madrona branch that blew down overnight, while Elana watches, hands on her hips. I don't know where Andrew is.

After that the three of them disappear up the driveway, looking for other downed limbs, so it's just me and Grandma at breakfast, and this morning Grandma has something special. Cottage cheese. I add a spoonful of huckleberry jam and stir the whole thing up Valentine pink. It tastes exactly like I feel.

After breakfast Grandma opens the refrigerator and takes out something large wrapped in cloth. It's the salmon Andrew smoked the day before. She hands it to me. "For Mom and Dad." Then

Grandma wipes her hand on a faded red-and-white tea towel and flips it over her shoulder. She hugs me, a long squeeze, my nose is pressed against the damp towel. I breathe in the smell of it, try to press it into memory.

"I'll see you soon, Grandma."

"Very soon." She turns. "I have applesauce to make."

Carrying the salmon across both arms like a baby, I wedge myself through the sliding glass door shoulder first and walk across Grandma's lawn toward the boat.

I never noticed before how white our boat is. It's like someone was out there polishing it in the night. I climb aboard, stow the salmon in my backpack, and begin putting up the sails. It takes me maybe ten or fifteen minutes to tie everything, then I pull the cord and the engine fires up. That feels lucky.

Next, I bend my waist over the side of the boat and unhook the rope from the dock cleat. I lay it carefully loop by loop in a neat pile. Lastly, I pull Dad's eyeglasses out of my sweatshirt pocket and set them next to the steering wheel, where there is a cup holder.

I set my hands tentatively on the wheel and think about how to move back and away from the dock. I get the feeling that Andrew is just off to one side--in the shade near the chicken coop maybe--staring as usual. But then curiosity gets to be too much and I look. It's not Andrew watching but Grandma. Jaden, Eric, and Elana are standing on the porch too. Everyone but Andrew. Not surprising.

They wave, and I wave back, but my gaze lingers on Grandma. I can see the red-and-white towel still over her shoulder. She blows me a kiss like I'm a little kid. Then I push my foot down on the gas pedal, underneath me the engine roars, and I'm off.

Once I am turned around from the dock, I switch the motor off. The sails take a moment to find the wind, but then snap and billow proudly. I do nothing but sit on the bench and watch the north shore of Grandma's bay slide slowly past. Trees and leaves, sand and seaweed, rocks and moss, and dirt. A million shades of green to gray to blue to brown.

After what might have been an hour, the bay opens up, the shoreline slips back and disappears, and in front of me McNeil and Anderson glide into place. This is where Andrew and I came with the crab pots.

I fiddle with the compass for a while, trying to get the nose of the boat to line up perfectly with the *SE* mark, but it's not solid ground like in the woods yesterday, and the arrow jumps around so much it's impossible, so I give up and stroll back to the bench.

Jaden said a small boat like mine can get a bit off course and then back on course quickly.

Kneeling, I wrap my hands around the metal cord railing and hang over it, bending at the waist to see how close I can get to the water. Close enough to get spray up my nostrils, it turns out. I pull myself up, wipe my face on my shirt, and go back down. This time I'm so far over my feet kick straight up in the air. I am completely upside down beside the boat. The top of my head is submerged. I hold myself back with tight fists.

All around the boat the sun flashes against the small waves, searing white spots into my vision. Closer up, the sun cuts through the water, visible for about a foot down. I stare down, imagining what would happen if I let go and dove head first to the bottom of the ocean.

Despite all the legends about giant squid taking down ships, in real life the giant octopus aren't like that at all. They are shy and smart. They notice everything, but keep to themselves. The giant squid in *Harry Potter* is always helping out students who fall into the lake. I think a giant octopus would be friendly if it could talk.

In fact, I am thinking, as I flip myself over the side again and hang upside down over Puget Sound, I could learn to get along with the octopus under the bridge. I am shy. I am smart. I notice things and keep to myself. Except for the fact that I can't breathe water and he can't breathe air, I think the octopus and I have a lot in common. I think I would like him.

After a while I pop back up and walk back to the wheel, rolling out the ache in my shoulders. I am close enough to Anderson Island that I can see people moving around inside their houses. Someone is standing near a giant window with their hand on what looks like the back of a couch, or a table. Another person is going from room to room, picking things up off the floor.

Grandma told me to smile, so I do, until I decide that wandering around in a boat by myself smiling all the time looks suspicious, and anyway my cheeks are sore, so I drop it.

Time passes quiet and peaceful. Anderson Island slides behind and in the distance I can make out a thin strip of purple that must be Steilacoom. Lunch sounds good, so I go below into the cabin where Elana has stashed the cooler and dig around through the carefully wrapped packages.

As much as I would like to break off a big chunk of smoked salmon for myself, I imagine how I would feel giving the rest to Mom and Dad, so instead I take one hard boiled egg and one long, well-scrubbed carrot, and save everything else. I pour myself a mug of water from the canteen and carry my lunch back up the stairs to eat.

I've already tossed the eggshell in the water and am carefully nibbling at the white part, leaving the yolk untouched in the center like a rising sun, when I hear it. A low hoot. The train. Sure enough, I can see a long black worm underlining Steilacoom.

I smile, a real smile this time, and think of Grandma, imagine her standing at her sink peeling apples and listening to the train whistle, too. Thinking of me at the exact same moment I am thinking of her.

Then Sarah pops into my mind, out of nowhere once again, as if it's her, not me, in control of what I'm thinking. In my mind she is describing California. She's telling me about the beaches with sand so white it hurts your eyes. Palm trees that *shush* in the wind. The smell of citrus everywhere.

I wonder if I could describe Washington in a way that makes it sound as beautiful as California. It's cold and rainy eight or nine months out of the year here, and when it's not raining everything's so dry it's crisp. Still, the trees are tall, and the Sound is peaceful, and in May, when it finally stops raining, all the flowers come out, and it warms up, and it turns into one of the most wonderful places in the world.

I wonder if all places in the world are naturally beautiful in their own way, or if there are some places that are just plain ugly. Maybe everyone believes the place they come from is most beautiful, while in reality no place is better than any other.

I pour a second mug of water, swallow it all in one long drink, then wipe my mouth with the back of my sleeve and set the mug in the cupholder. After that, for no real reason, my eyes fall on a thick steel chain that is hanging loose beside the cabin. I sort of rest my eyes there and let them ride up and down the shiny side of the metal for a full minute before it occurs to me that anything is wrong.

The gas is gone.

That's the place where I watched Elana lock up the gas can yesterday, the one with three whole gallons Grandma had been saving. She hauled it out, wrapped the chain through the handle on the side of the can, snapped a padlock around two links, and strung the key onto my keychain. I drop to my knees to examine my keychain dangling from the ignition. The key's also gone.

There have been times in my life when I doubted my own memories, when I told myself stories about things that I wished were true so much I started to believe them, but this is not one of those times. I very clearly remember last night sitting in just this spot on this bench watching Elana lock up the gas can. I remember because I was wondering if it was the sort of thing I really ought to be doing myself, and thinking I was getting a little old to just sit and watch an adult do things for me, even when they seemed happy to do it.

But who took my gas? And why?

After that, any momentary happiness I felt disappeared with the breeze. I grip the steering wheel, aware of every tiny bounce of waves underfoot, every creak of wood, willing the boat to move faster. The fuel gauge indicator is pointing to the second horizontal bar of the big red E.

There is only one thing I can think of to do. Ask Dad.

Over the next couple hours a sharp pain forms in the temple on the right side of my head, a pulsing, throbbing ache, making my eyes run when the sun's glare reflects up off the water. I stand still as a bird-of-prey, staring north, waiting for the Narrows Bridge to appear.

Grandma was right. It is farther than it looks on the map. As the boat rounds each bend in the coastline I convince myself the bridge will pop into view. Each time it doesn't, I feel let down, as if there is a battle between me and geography, and I'm losing.

A wild thought hits. What if someone blew up the bridge? If so, I may already be well on my way to Seattle. I have not and never will want to travel all the way to Seattle.

Why is it that happiness seems to come in tiny snips, but anxiety lingers?

But then, finally, in the distance, I see Tent City. I smell it before I see it, actually. The smoke catches the back of my throat and stings. My eyes water.

When I'm closer up I see people. Twenty, twenty-five, maybe as much thirty people running back and forth around big flaming piles. Kids, it looks like, teenagers maybe, judging by their energy. A joyful hoot skids across the water.

They're burning tires. I watch an older boy roll one down a hill and chase after it as it picks up speed. There are five or six big piles of tires, and from the top of each one comes billowing plumes of oily black smoke.

There aren't many tires left, so burning them is a waste. You can stack them up and plant potatoes. You can make other things with them.

Once Dad came across a bunch of tires in a marsh he was surveying with his students. He got each student to dig out one tire each, and when they were done surveying they rolled all the tires to our house, a muddy procession all the way down our street, and they stacked them in wobbly towers beside our compost pile. Dad used the tires to build the backyard swing set for me, with a bridge and a climbing wall, although that was years ago and now it's mostly Flossie's.

At least an hour passes after Tent City is behind me and before the Narrows Bridge appears. More than anything I want to lift off the boat and fly to it, fly straight up over the bridge, then circle it a bit and perch on top of one of its graceful swooping cables. Survey the city from above. Like Birdman.

Finally I see Day Island and the marina, too. Most of the boats are gone, like Grandma said. Where did they go? How did she know they'd be gone?

I climb fore to aft rolling up sails. Hand over hand, I maneuver the big boat into the small slip. It is quiet here. I mean, it's always pretty quiet at the marina, but today it feels deserted. The shouts from Tent City are the last human sounds I heard. I get a feeling that even as I perk up my ears, listening to the city, in some impossible way it's also listening to me.

Once I've motored into a spot, the fuel gauge indicator arrow is sunk all the way to the bottom of *E*. I have nothing left to motor out again. Doesn't matter. Dad will find gas. The rope uncoils easily and I grab the dock and secure the boat to the metal cleat. Then I jump down into the cabin and zip around locking things up. I grab the backpack with the salmon and other food. I double check every lock. I grab Dad's glasses.

I sling the backpack over two arms and tighten the straps. Then I climb off the boat onto the dock, picture myself being swept up into one of Dad's rib-crunching hugs, take a deep breath, and walk.

Chapter Ten: Home Again

There isn't anyone, as far as I can tell, at the marina. There isn't anyone working on a boat, or tying up, or just standing around talking either. It's so quiet I can hear the sound of a seagull's feathers moving over each other as he swoops toward the dock.

I take wide steps across the ancient parking lot, spent dandelions puffing in my wake, then past the rusted metal posts where a chain link fence used to be. I take the 19th Street hill behind it quickly, too, not running but walking fast, trying to think only about home.

All the way up 19th Street I don't see a single person. All the houses have their curtains down, and a lot of them have long wooden boards nailed across the windows too. These are what they used to call view homes. It was a long time before I realized they were called that because of the views people got looking out of them, not the views of people looking at them from outside.

It's weird to see them boarded up like everyone's gone away.

Then, at the corner, where 19th intersects with Fernside Drive, where I need to cross the street and take a left to cut north to Sixth, a door opens. An old man raps his cane against the door. "Stupid kid! Ain't you heard? McAllister's dead."

I take a step toward his house. "Just now? The president died just now?"

"State of emergency!" He slams the door.

I keep walking, keep imagining myself already at home. Somewhere far in the distance there is a patter of shots, then again from somewhere else behind, like birds calling. Right at this moment all over the city, people are finding out that President McAllister is dead.

Shattered glass on the pavement shines like fallen stars. What a sound it must have made while breaking. There's other stuff, too. Cast iron pots and bookshelves, a broom, winter coats and filing cabinets, a radio, a laundry basket, jewelry boxes, bath mats and an old broken rake. Like a crazy person is having a yard sale.

Further down the street a wooden dollhouse is flung on its side, blocking the steps to the real house. Miniature chairs and tables and other furniture are scattered everywhere, not even broken yet. I step carefully over a tiny dresser with a tiny oval mirror. It makes me think, of course, about Flossie and how she is about her stuff, especially Zebra.

A couple blocks before the Kmart, where the road goes under what used to be Highway 16, there's a smear of something dark on the road, and when I get closer I see its blood.

A dog was killed here, I tell myself.

A minute later, as if summoned by the power of my mind, three dogs slip out from a concrete pillar and head toward my bag, sniffing. They aren't barking and they don't look mean, exactly, but their fur is dusty and matted, in pursuit of their next meal.

"Bad dogs," I say in a half-whisper, not too quiet but not too loud. "Go home." They ignore me. I can't blame them. They aren't being bad, just hungry. They smell salmon. And they probably have no home to go to anyway.

I give a low growl, bend way down and glare at each one of them in the eye, pull up my lips, bare my teeth and growl again.

I stand there, half bent over, frozen and glaring. It works. After a minute it actually works. They back off at least, sniff around at the ground, glancing shyly at me, then away. Finally I straighten up and walk. They hang back a few feet, but they're still trailing me. I don't turn around but I can hear their claws on the pavement.

At first I hope my canine entourage will get bored and wander off, but then I change my mind. I like them. I'm far enough from the marina now that I decide to drop the story about the Anderson Island church camp and tell anyone who asks that I am taking my dogs out hunting. Then I will snarl like I am more comfortable with dogs than people and start reaching into my bag really slow, like they ought to be afraid of what I will pull out of there.

But block after block the dogs and I are the only show around, and I start to feel less scared. Walking does that. Just putting one foot in front of another and reducing the space between me and home does something to my mind.

At the corner of Fernside and Sixth there's an overgrown lot that usually has tents and mattresses and junk everywhere. It has always given me a creepy feeling. I imagine it must be taken over by Phoenix now, so when I get to the end of Fernside I cross the street and sprint for two whole blocks until I'm gasping.

After that, catching my breath, I walk the part of Sixth that is all businesses, no houses, which is good because the buildings are farther back from the road, behind parking lots, and it seems unlikely that someone could pop out in front of me.

The Kmart is deserted. No black car anywhere. It looks kind of sad sitting there all by itself inside a big, empty parking lot. Nobody running into a friend they hadn't seen in a while, nobody hauling a week's worth of bacon and veggies home, no kids outside playing kickball on what's left of the pavement.

Two blocks past the Kmart I can see the blue front porch of Chase's house.

Will I have time to visit while I'm here? Even if I do have time, will Mom and Dad let me? I would really like to see Chase try and stick his fingers in a jar of crab bait. I bet he couldn't! I am wondering if there is a way to get some while I'm here. I could buy some from the guy who sells crab door-to-door, maybe.

I am so caught up imagining Chase and a jar of crab bait that the scene at the Messerman house is like being woken up from a dream.

The front door is gone. Windows too. The brick-color curtains that hang in the living room flap out toward the street. There is blood on the front walk.

After that it is almost a relief to see boards up but no damage to our home. Still, it is ugly. Sad. Although I had been seeing boarded up houses all the way from the marina, none of the boards look so out of place and wrong as the boards across our house do.

At least we haven't been looted.

But how will I ever get in?

The front door is covered by a large sheet of wood, something Dad must have found at work because it has the name and address of the community college printed in red. Two-by-fours like a treehouse ladder cover each window. The lights are off. The curtains drawn. Nothing to see inside, same as everywhere.

    I turn around and bend down again to the dogs, growl, and then stand up and make a few ridiculous karate chops in their direction, moves I've seen other kids do. The middle dog whimpers and lies down, then the other two do as well, heads on their paws, eyes on me. Three filthy lumps filling up our front walk.

    Leaving them with my best glare, I step up to the front door on light feet, skipping the stair where the board creaks. I stand there, a stranger at my own door, wondering what to do next. I knock, three gentle knocks, and wait. The noise of my knocking seems amplified. I picture old Mr. Allen picking his way to the front door, the Messerman kids racing each other to theirs, even the guy with the cars in his yard peeking out.

    There is no response. No movement of shadows behind curtains. No sound. Nothing. I knock again, louder this time.

    Nothing.

    Could they have left? Maybe things got even worse and there's no one inside the house. What if, their plans changed between the time Grandma called and I arrived on the porch. What if they had to flee?

If so, where would they go? How would I find them? How would I get there?

I plunk down cross-legged in front of the door to think.

There's a noise behind me. At first I think it's an animal. Maybe a bird pecking. A gentle *rat-tat-tat*, like a key tapping on glass. I turn and see the window curtains, the window above the stairs, has parted, just an inch. Fast as I can, bringing the dogs to their feet, I jump up and peer in. In the space where the curtains have parted, someone--Mom? Dad?--is holding a scrap of paper against the glass. Something has been written on it in very small letters. I lean in.

Basement window.

Stepping quietly, I make my way through the tall grass of the yard, unhook the gate and snap it closed behind me, leaving the dogs on the other side. The basement windows--there are two short windows about six inches off the ground--are also boarded up.

What am I supposed to do? I don't have the tools to pull off the boards myself. Don't have the strength, either.

I get down on my hands and knees and look closely. I wedge a thumb behind one board and it pops right off in my hands. Turning the wood over, I see Dad's used short nails, maybe a quarter-inch longer than the wood is thick. The second board pops off just as quick. I set the boards in the grass, and slide the basement window open so there is room for me to wiggle inside.

I slide in feet first on my belly, lowering myself, then sort of half-turn and jump, landing on Dad's cluttered workbench and somehow not twisting an ankle. I reach up and pull the backpack in behind me.

When I turn around Mom and Dad are standing there, still as deer. No one, not one of us, says a word. Dad takes a couple steps forward, puts his arms out, and I do, too. Then all at once my legs go boneless, just turn into jelly underneath me. My knees buckle and I sort of collapse into Dad's arms and he catches me.

And it's just like I imagined. He's squeezing tight, so tight I can't even breathe. But at the same time I'm hoping he'll never let me go.

Chapter Eleven:
Through the Eye of the Storm

    Dad sets the boards back in place and joins Mom and me. I don't know how long we stay there, the three of us cross legged on the floor in the basement. I am talking so fast I keep running out of breath, filling them in on everything. The bacon Grandma cooks every morning, the rake I used to harvest huckleberries, Andrew, who used to live by Kendra. Jaden and the compass practice, and Dad in high school. I tell them about how Grandma had me cleaning up after the chickens, scraping out the poop and hauling it off to compost. I tell them about gathering eggs--some still warm from the chicken's butt! That makes them laugh. I tell them about crabbing.

    I don't know if telling them about rotten fish for bait will turn them off crab for the rest of their lives, but I tell them about that, too.

    Dad nods. They knew.

"You knew, and you still ate crab?"

"There are a lot of foods, once you know how they are made, you wish you didn't know," Mom says.

"Farming is real life," Dad says, drawing a circle in the air with his finger. "And death too. All of it, the whole cycle."

I nod. Then I remember my gifts for them and reach for the backpack. First the salmon. I hand it to Mom.

"What's this?" she says. She lifts up one edge of the cloth and smiles, hugging it to her chest. "How thoughtful, Jay," she says. "We'll enjoy this very much. Thank you."

"It's really from Grandma."

"Tell Grandma thank you then."

I nod. "Dogs followed me here," I say. "They could smell it."

"I could smell it, too," Dad says.

Everyone laughs.

"There's something for you too Dad." I zip the main pocket of the backpack closed again and tip it back so I can get into the small pocket in the front. The reason I didn't think of the glasses sooner is because he's wearing another pair.

I wish for a moment that there was some kind of cloth to wrap the glasses in too, something to make it seem more like a present, but there isn't, so I just pull the glasses out of my backpack real quick and hand them over.

"These are mine?" he says, looking at the spot where he's scratched his initials. "Really? How in the world? Oh Jay!" He takes off the spare pair and lets them drop to his lap. Then he puts the ones I've brought on and says "Oh," again, looking around, blinking and moving his head around to look at things near and far. "Thank you! Thank you!"

I open my mouth to ask what happened, how he lost them, and whether Andrew was there, but I see Mom frowning. I'll ask later.

Mom leans in and examines the glasses. "Fingerprints?" she says. "Here, give them to me." Dad takes the glasses off, folds the arms in and hands them over. Mom disappears up the stairs to wash them.

I picked only the best things to tell Mom and Dad. I see myself stepping on Andrew's shoelace, arguing with Grandma about crab bait. Is leaving things out the same as telling a lie? If so, Dad's been lying to me about his other work for my whole life.

"I know about everything now," I say.

Dad's eyebrows go up. "From living on the farm?"

"No. Well, that too. I mean I know all about you. The work you do while I'm at school." I lean in and drop my voice to a whisper. "*Collectivists.*"

Dad blinks. Without his glasses, he looks different. Pale. His eyes seem small and unprotected.

He reminds me of some kind of underground rodent. "I was going to tell you when I found the right time."

In fourteen years he hadn't found the right time?

"You had time."

Dad doesn't say anything. He glances at me, eyebrows up, surprised, but he doesn't deny it. I don't say anything either, although in a way I would very much like to fill in the silence with more nice details about Grandma's house, with anything, just to shove something into the space between my mean words and me.

On the far side of the basement where the window's been boarded up again I see a single dim ray of sun spotlighting a pile of sawdust on dad's workbench. Everything else looks blue. Shadows are blue. How come I've never noticed that shadows are blue?

I want to tell Dad I don't mind. That I feel proud of him actually, proud to have him as a father, doing all this important work, and I don't care that people misunderstand the Collectivist ideas. But at the same time, I don't know if that's really how I feel. Right at this moment I wish there didn't have to be secrets.

I wish--part of me wishes--that I was born a Messerman. Twin brother to Chase. A member of a plain old regular Tacoma family, with no secrets to hide or other work to do. I would be the quiet Messerman, the one who did not grab Sarah's backpack or goof off to the teacher. The one who nobody noticed at first, but eventually everyone loved.

"And that's the reason you can't go stay at Grandma's with us? With the way things are now, with the president--"

"He died just a couple hours ago."

"I know."

"With so much uncertainty, we have more work to do than ever, preparing shipments to Collectivists groups. There are several on and around the peninsula these days, which is exciting. We live in an amazing part of the world, don't we? Walk down the road and you wouldn't think there was anyone else living there, but the woods are so thick and trees grow so fast they make excellent privacy, and--"

"I know, Dad." I stand, put my hands on my hips and bend backward to stretch. "Can we go upstairs?"

Dad ignores me. "What I was going to say was I am working on your mom. About me going with you, I mean. I want to go very much. We have talked and talked about it, and she's finally warming up to the idea. Problem is she does not feel comfortable taking on my responsibilities. I understand that. They have never worked together directly, your mom and Kendra. Your mom is a behind-the-scenes sort of person, and the plan was always to keep her that way."

My heart leaps. "You're going to Grandma's with me and Flossie?"

"I may. Let me keep talking to Mom, she'll come around. Don't say anything to Flossie yet."

"Where is Flossie?"

"Asleep on the couch."

"Grandma said she doesn't sleep."

"She doesn't, really. Go up there. You'll see what I mean."

"Why isn't she in her bedroom?"

"She refuses. She says she doesn't like to be upstairs. She won't even use the bathroom without your mother going in and sitting right beside her while she does." He laughs.

"Why won't she sleep in her bedroom?"

"Who knows? She developed all sorts of strange fears after the close call she had at school." He pauses. "Did Grandma tell you?"

"Yes."

"Well, first her brother leaves, and then that happens. Kind of a one-two punch. Then, add to it, the sounds we've been hearing outside." Dad gets quiet, and my mind flashes on the blood I saw. *Just a dog.* "Altogether it seems it was too much for her."

Dad drops his head and looks at his hands in his lap.

"Well," I say, straightening up, "I didn't see anyone on my walk in. One old man on his porch. Otherwise not a soul. Everyone's windows are boarded up, curtains drawn, not a sound anywhere, no movement. It's like everyone's gone away."

Dad nods. "It's the gloom. That's what's getting to the three of us. There's so little light inside the house with these boards up. We're living in eternal twilight. It does something to a person."

"So why isn't anybody outside? I know it's a state of emergency, but no one's enforcing it, so who cares?"

"Jay, people are getting killed outside."

"Are you sure? Do you know that for a fact? I had a very peaceful walk here."

"Angels followed you."

I turn. Mom's standing at the bottom of the staircase with Dad's cleaned glasses. I hadn't heard her come down.

"You were just lucky," Dad says, taking the glasses from her and settling them on his face. "The electricity hasn't been on since the day you left, which is why you didn't see lights. You walked through the eye of the storm and came out without a scratch. Doesn't mean you'll be so lucky on the way out."

"You remember Mrs. Messerman?" Mom asks.

"Chase's mom?"

"The other Mrs. Messerman. Chase's grandma."

"The one who always brings us her overgrown zucchini? What about her?"

"They got her."

I swallow. "They *got* her? What does that mean?"

"Chase's dad found her. She was… She had been shot to death behind her house. He's a wreck." Mom, standing behind me now, wraps her arms around my chest and kisses the top of my head. In my memory Mrs. Messerman hobbles up the Messerman's front walk. Then I see her face down on her patio, a blood red as a rose across her back. I shiver. "The rest of the family fled."

"Is that why…." I trail off.

"Yes."

"Do you want to see your sister?" Dad says after a minute. "She'd like to see you."

The three of us walk up the wooden stairs that lead up to the kitchen. I set my bag on a chair at the table, take off my shoes, and step quietly into the living room.

Flossie is asleep on the couch. A clump of hair is a floppy *J* plastered to her forehead. Her cheeks are pale, but underneath and around her eyes is dark, sort of purplish. I can see thin blue veins on her eyelids, thicker ones on her neck. Mom or Dad has placed a quilt over her, and she seems to disappear into the couch underneath it, a landscape of patchwork farmland, only one arm visible. Her fingers twitch.

"How long has she been asleep?" I ask.

"Not long," Dad says. "An hour. It's about as long as she'll go."

"We keep her in our bedroom with us at night," Mom says. "She wanders all around, opening drawers, playing. She keeps us up, but at least we know she isn't hurting herself."

The three of us stand there staring at Flossie like she's a piece of art we're trying to understand.

Flossie tosses her head from one side to another and gives a mournful sob.

"She's having a nightmare?"

Mom nods. "She's always having a nightmare."

Just then Flossie's eyes pop open. She stares intently at the ceiling, then blinks. Her eyebrows drop and her chin wrinkles, ready to sob. I've never seen anyone wake up looking so exhausted.

Mom goes to her first, on her knees, with a kiss. "I have a surprise for you."

Flossie sits up. Mom pats her back. "What is it?" Flossie's voice is deep.

"Your brother is here."

Flossie stares at her, as if deciding whether or not this is some sort of trick, then cranes her neck to see behind. "Jay? Where?"

I step out from the doorway. "Surprise!" I say brightly, kneeling down and wrapping my arms around her tiny body. She hugs me tighter than I would have thought, practically hanging from my shoulders. Her hair feels greasy and her head smells sour. There's a damp, clammy feeling to her skin, and when we pull apart I can feel her cheek peeling away from my cheek but I don't mind.

Flossie turns to Mom. "Am I dreaming?"

Mom laughs. "No."

"I didn't think so," Flossie puts her eyes back on me. The skin on her lips has divided, like sections on a worm, where she's been licking it.

Mom asks if I'm hungry. I am. She goes to the kitchen.

"Are you packed?" I ask Flossie.

"Packed for what?" Flossie says.

On the other side of the couch, Dad shakes his head. "We hadn't told her. We wanted to be sure, you know, that she wouldn't be disappointed."

I get what he means. He wanted to make sure I made it here alive.

"Where are we going?" Flossie asks again.

"I'll tell you when we get upstairs."

"Good luck with that." Dad grins.

I look at Flossie. "You want to know where we're going, don't you?"

Flossie gives a slow nod.

"Then you'll have to follow me into your room to find out."

And, easy as that, I get Flossie back into her own bedroom for the first time in a week.

Chapter Twelve: Midnight Monopoly

Dinner that night is beans from a can. A scoop of peas, also from a can, all by themselves in a bowl. There's six pieces of bacon to share, which we eat first. Even Flossie eats a little, nibbling doll-sized pieces between tremendous sighs.

This is celebration food, stuff Mom usually pulls out only on holidays. But today no one is celebrating.

The beans are good, and the bacon of course, but the peas squash into a metallic paste in my mouth. There's also powdered milk, which is terrible.

Earlier, Mom and Dad were talking in the kitchen while I was upstairs helping Flossie pack her bag, and I can't help wondering if Dad's managed to convince Mom to let him go with us yet. I bet if he had he'd bring it up himself, so I keep quiet but look at him once or twice expectantly like maybe he knows what I am hoping he will say. But Dad just keeps putting food in his mouth and smiling at everyone like we are a normal family eating a normal dinner on a normal day.

I decide it's time to break it to them about the missing gas.

"It was there last night and it was gone this morning. I'm positive. One hundred percent. Trust me it's not still sitting on Grandma's dock. I remember watching Elana lock it up." I glance at Dad. He is frowning at his plate. "And I don't think they're selling gas at the gas station anymore."

"I'm sure they're not," Mom says.

"What do you think you should do?" Dad asks

"I asked you because I don't know!

"But what do you *think*?"

"How about that gas station on the way to the marina? Do you think they have gas?"

"No," Dad says, setting down his fork. "I don't think they do. Gas or no gas, we are sailing out tomorrow. First thing, early. I'll sleep on it," he smiles and wrinkles his nose, sliding up his glasses. "Something will come to me."

***

That night, later, I don't know what time exactly, a noise makes my eyes open. A hundred cymbals crashing at once. Glass breaking. I'm so wide-awake I could roll over and start solving equations like it was the middle of math class.

After a few minutes lying in bed waiting for another crash I get up, get dressed, and go downstairs. Dad is standing at the window beside the front door, his nose pressed to the inch where he's pulled the curtains apart.

Dad sees me and moves aside without a word, waves me to the curtains. I don't see anything. Then, after scrolling my eyes back and forth along the road, I do. Someone is walking. A thin, single figure, dressed all in black, is walking silently down the road past our house. He has a black cloth wrapped over his nose and mouth.

It is hard to see him. That's what gets me. Even though it's night, the sky is clear and a bright moon, nearly full, there are plenty of spots for him to disappear, and he does. All along our street are leafy maple trees, close enough together to form a canopy over the sidewalk. I used to stand on the porch and imagine climbing them, jumping from tree to tree like a squirrel. I did climb them, many times, up to a year or two ago. I used to believe they were planted there just for me.

Squirrels. Why would something so dumb pop into my head right now?

I see the way he's using the trees for cover, his silhouette melting into the shadows as he pauses beside each trunk to scope out the houses around him. If I don't keep my eyes on the spot where he is, I lose him and have to search around again.

He slips into a garage--it's the family with the arugula-thief chickens. He doesn't come out for a long time. I figure I must have missed him, or he took a back door and went out through the alley.

Then, from the far side of our yard where it is difficult to see from our window, I see a second person. Shorter, same dark clothes, just as thin.

He had been even closer than the first guy the whole time, but I hadn't even seen him.

The first man's out of the garage again, silent as can be, only this time I can see he's got something in his hands. When he gets closer I see what it is. A glass jug, the gallon size to store water in. He's also swinging some kind of chain.

"Quiet now," Dad breathes over my shoulder. I don't know why, because I haven't said anything, although I was thinking of asking what the guy would want a glass jug for. He's getting closer to our house. "If we stay still, he can't see us."

All at once the guy is directly in front of our house. He's facing us, only twelve feet, maybe ten, from Dad and me, right there under the enormous split-trunk maple where I have stood myself a thousand times, played, daydreamed, strolled round and round in lazy circles, waiting for Flossie to hurry up so we can walk to school.

I watch how he keeps his head and body still. Only his eyes move, sliding up and around the front of our house, taking in the boarded up door, the windows with their ladder slats. A lizard catching a fly.

A cold feeling creeps across my skin, raising the hairs on my arms and legs. At the same time, I can feel my forehead starting to sweat.

The giant Pacific octopus rarely lives in its den for more than a month. Once it leaves, another octopus moves in. Who will move into our house when Dad, Mom, Flossie and I move out? Who has moved into Sarah's house in California?

It seems he stands there an hour, lizard eyes all over our house.

The second one doesn't hesitate. Head down, legs pumping, he heads for his target like an angry hornet, and within five seconds he has both the glass jug and the chain in his hands. The first guy never saw it coming. He throws an arm around his neck and almost knocks him off his feet, but the thief bows his head, slips out of the chokehold and is halfway down the block before the first guy even starts running.

All of this in silence.

Dad slides the curtain shut and smiles like it was a good show. "Monopoly?"

An hour later, Dad has houses on both Park Place and Broadway and is watching me turn my real estate cards face down to pay the rent I owe him. "So I bet you want to know what happened to me back on the road the other day," he starts, wiggling his nose. "About my glasses?"

I nod.

Dad holds up three fingers. "Three guys. They had been waiting in the woods and stepped out all at once from three different spots. Well-coordinated. I am not a military strategist but I seem to remember hearing U.S. forces always go in three-to-one. Most people cannot fight off three at once."

"You had to fight them?"

"Well, not exactly. Nobody threw any punches."

"So what happened?"

"They wanted information. They tried to intimidate me into giving it."

"Information about what?"

Dad shrugs and looks behind me into the dark living room. "Collectivist colonies. People we work with both on and off the peninsula. Locations, names, anything I'd give them," he shakes his head. "They got nothing."

"How did they know who you are? How did they know when you would be walking by?"

"Do not know and do not know. I've been puzzling over it ever since."

"What did they look like?"

Dad frowns. "One was tall. Very tall and thin, with his head shaved bald. The other two were blond and curly. Maybe brothers."

"Brothers? Are you sure?"

"Not sure. No one I recognized. Why?"

Blond and curly brothers. That's Andrew. And Patrick.

I had my suspicions, but the truth is hot as fire. I get all creepy-crawly then, imagining Andrew back at Grandma's, feeding the chickens, picking the huckleberries, and her without any idea what he's up to. Even so, I can't say it out loud. Maybe doing so would help Dad but instead I feel like not telling is safer. "No reason," I say. "Just trying to get the details right."

Dad leans in to whisper as if we are in danger of being overheard. He smiles. "I know I look like a wimp. Don't worry. It's all part of the master plan."

I scoop up the dice and let them click against each other in my palms, then toss them on the board and count off my spaces.

"Did you get Mom to come around?"

"Come around how?"

"About you going with us."

"Oh, that." Dad shakes the dice in his palm and drops them on the table. I watch him count eleven spaces with his top hat token then plunk down $100 for property tax in the center of the board.

When his turn is finished he clears his throat and flashes a smile. "Yep. No problem. I'm going."

Could it really be that easy?

An hour later, Mom comes downstairs, points to the living room, and in a scratchy voice charges Dad and me with folding the clothes she washed yesterday.

Without electricity, we're washing by hand, with a bucket. That's how I've watched Grandma wash clothes all week, but Mom doesn't have a bumpy metal washboard like Grandma does, to rub the stains out, or the wringer Grandma puts clothes through to squeeze out the water. Instead, Mom's squeezed them out the best she can and hung the clothes up on a set of wooden dowels that fold out from the wall above the wood stove. The boarded-up house is still warm enough that clothes will probably dry, even though the wood stove isn't on.

I take a dishcloth off a dowel, tug each corner to soften the stiff fabric, fold it in fourths and stack it.

Dad is talking about the guy we saw earlier. He's glad we saw him. That way, he says, we'll know what to look out for. "It's the lone wolves that get me. I know you don't want to believe this, that it's easier to believe it was divine intervention or whatever your mother was talking about last night, but the truth is that the streets are filled with guys like him, night and day. Phoenix rule. Not much for old guys like me to do anymore but stand and watch. It's just dumb luck that you didn't run into one of them yesterday."

I let his words roll around a minute in my mind. *Dumb luck*. How can it be that dumb luck is the same thing as good luck, when *dumb* and *good* mean such different things?

Maybe they are different. Maybe *dumb* luck is what you have when you're too dumb to know you are lucky.

And maybe, now that I do know, I can't be lucky anymore.

"What about the black car?"

"What about it?"

"If we see it? What should we do?"

"Didn't I tell you?" Dad frowns and wiggles his nose. "Don't worry about the black car. It's stuck."

"It is?"

Dad nods. "Over by the freeway. I didn't actually see it myself, but your mom was telling me about it. Happened just a day or two ago. She heard a car engine in the distance on her way to Kmart, followed the sound, and saw it. Looked just like the one you described. Tinted windows. Chromium everything. It has to be the same car."

He shakes his head. "Karma."

When the clothes are all folded and stacked Dad tells me his plan to get gas.

"You remember Kendra?"

"Kendra." I say. "She has gas?"

Dad nods. "She'll either have some or know where to find some."

What I remember about Kendra is her kitchen. The cabinets were always stuffed full of food. There were herbs drying in bundles from the ceiling. There was dried meat. Dried fish. Dried fruit. There were bags of grain and beans. There were jars filled with pickled eggs in gray liquid and a whole bunch of other jars filled with other foods, carefully labeled. And it wasn't just the kitchen, either. Kendra's whole house was filled with stuff. My mind clicks. "She's one of them. A Collectivist. She works with you, doesn't she?"

Dad's mouth is a straight line. "Is. Was. Yes. People who support the movement drop off things at her house. Anything people might need. It's my job to fill the orders and send them out. That had been my job, I mean." He takes a breath. "What will they call Before when the way we used to live becomes the new Before?"

Another hour passes before we're ready to leave. Mom's in a frenzy. I wave away the can of peas she offers for my trip back, but she manages to slip in a box of powdered milk, beef jerky and another can of beans in sauce like we ate last night.

Mom wants me to take some of the smoked salmon for our trip back because she knows it's my favorite. But I remind her about the dogs. I tell her to keep it for herself like Grandma wanted, but Dad digs around in the back of a cabinet we never use, and after a minute pulls out a half-dozen ancient Ziplock bags.

He pops open a bag, breaks off a fist-size chunk of fish and slides it inside, then carefully presses out all the air from the bag with his fingers. He zips it closed, puts that bag inside another bag, presses the air out again and zips it. One bag after another, zipping each one, transforming the salmon into an indistinguishable puff of plastic. When all the bags are gone he turns it over and over in his hands, sniffing deeply, then hands it to me.

Dad's canvas Army-style bag, stuffed full, leans beside the coat rack in the hallway. I keep waiting for Mom to say something about it, but either she hasn't noticed it or she's choosing not to.

"What about some oats, Jay?" Mom calls from the living room where she's brushing Flossie's hair. "I know you won't have a way to cook while you're traveling, but would Jody like some oats to have at her house?"

"Sure. That would be nice. I'll put some in a container."

Flossie squeals like prodded livestock with every stroke of the hairbrush.

"Stop your bellyaching. I'm trying to help you," Mom says.

"You call it helping, I call it hurting."

Dad steps in from the hallway, bending down to look under the couch. "Anyone seen my boots?"

Mom stops brushing and looks at him. "You don't need your boots, because you're not going."

"Is that what we decided? In the end I thought we had it the other way."

Mom holds the hairbrush in two hands in her lap and bows her head. Flossie, sensing freedom, bounds off the couch and stands by the window like a mistreated cat.

"Call off the search party, the missing boots have been found!" Dad gets his boots from beside the bookshelf and sits down on the couch to put them on. "Sophia, we talked about it. I don't want to leave you all my responsibilities but I *can't* send our kids out there alone. You don't want the kids out there alone. I know you don't. It's a lose-lose."

Flossie laughs. "Loser! Loser!" she yells at Mom.

"Flossie!" Dad and I say at the same time.

Flossie shrugs.

Mom slaps the hairbrush against the palm of her other hand like a slow metronome. Her eyes are on Dad but she doesn't say anything. Dad has loosened up both of his boot laces and pulled back the tongues. He sticks his left foot in his boot and tugs the laces tight.

Mom holds out Flossie's hairbrush to me and I take it.

"Make her brush. Please." Her expression is stormy. Then she stands and goes quietly up the stairs, and we hear the creak of Mom and Dad's bed as she climbs into it.

The three of us file down to the basement.

I hoist Flossie up to the workbench--Dad's cleaned it off since I arrived--climb up myself and kneel down so my leg makes a sort of step. Flossie punches out the fake board with a gleeful shout, wriggles through in no time and skips away toward the tire swing. I shove my backpack onto the grass and climb out myself.

Then it's Dad's turn. He tosses the army bag out, and I reach over and scoop it off the grass, sit cross-legged with it in my lap. The fingers of his left hand work around the edge of the window, feeling for grip. His right elbow is braced against the other side. Dad hoists his head and shoulders onto the grass. He grins at me. Then there's a crash, a loud one, from inside, and all at once Dad slips back, reverses course, disappears from the window like there's some basement monster pulling him back in.

I jump to my knees and stick my head inside. Dad is on his back on the cement floor, the workbench on its side next to him.

The groan he's making tells me everything I need to know about whether or not he will be coming with us.

Mom comes clattering down two sets of stairs and drops to her knees beside Dad. She looks him over then picks up his hand and squeezes it to her chest. "I told you it was never part of the plan."

"There is no plan!" Dad yells.

Flossie thumps down next to me in the grass and sticks her head in the window.

"Dad? Are you okay?"

"I'll be fine. Just bruised."

"But you're still going, right? I'm not going if you're not going! I'll get kidnapped again!"

There is a pause. Dad takes a breath and lets it out slowly. "Flossie, Sweetheart, you are not the parent and you do not get to make these decisions. It looks like, I don't think-- I will not be able to go after all. But don't worry. Jay is going to be with you the whole time and he's going to make it impossible for anyone to--"

Dad stops talking because Flossie is on her belly about to nose-dive inside the basement. I grab hold of her legs, and inside the house Mom has her hands on Flossie's shoulders, and together the two of us slide her back into the yard.

"Plus, you're good at taking care of yourself. I happen to know you are one of the fastest runners in the city of Tacoma," I say, scooting myself between Flossie and the window in case she decides to try it again.

Flossie scowls. "*The* fastest runner." She looks from me to the window, where Mom's head and shoulders takes up all the space. Then I reach past her and pick up the boards with the too-short nails. She looks at it for a second in my hands. Then she sticks her head back in the window and speaks in a quiet voice. "Goodbye. I love you. Be safe." I shove Dad's bag back inside, place the board back on the window and push on it with my palms so it stays.

There is nothing more to say and nothing more to do, so I stand, swing my backpack over my shoulders, hold out my hand for Flossie, and we go.

Chapter Thirteen:
Do Not Tell Them Your Name

When we're out front of the house I hoist Flossie on to my waist. I pick her up facing me and she wraps her arms around my neck, legs around my waist, head tucked over one shoulder. Easier said than done. She's got long legs and I have to keep pulling clumps of her hair out of my mouth. But she stays still and she isn't heavy, not much heavier than my backpack after all the food Mom crammed into it. I do this so Flossie can keep an eye out behind while I am looking in front of us. If she sees anything, she's supposed to pinch my neck. We talked about it before we left. Dad said it was a good plan.

We walk fifteen blocks and not once does Flossie pinch my neck.

"Will Mom and Dad be safe at home, do you think?" Flossie asks out of nowhere.

"Sure they'll be safe. They've been safe all these years, haven't they?"

"How will they find us when it's time to come home again?"

"We'll be at Grandma's. They can walk or take a boat. Whatever they feel like doing."

This seems to satisfy Flossie. By the time we get close to Kendra's I feel pretty good. Like I have a certain specialness clinging to me, a lucky fringe. For the first time I stop thinking about where Phoenix might be hiding and start thinking about other things, Sarah mostly, but also what chores Jody will make Flossie do when she gets there.

But when we round the corner to Kendra's house I nearly drop my sister on the ground.

Kendra's house has been ransacked. Robbed. Looted. The windows are smashed. The front door hangs from one hinge. An ancient wooden computer hutch Kendra used as a writing desk is upside down on the front lawn, flung halfway across the flower bed. The kitchen table I spent many afternoons with a book on top of is out there, too.

Broken glass sparkles across the sidewalk and road. One wall has been hacked apart with what must have been an axe. There are a dozen wires poking out which someone didn't even bother to steal. There are at least thirty-five jelly jars on the sidewalk, leaking thick dark blackberry jam like slug slime. I just stand there, holding Flossie, taking it all in.

Flossie twists around in my arms to see why we've stopped, and sucks in her breath when she sees it. "Isn't this Kendra's house? Was she home when it happened?"

"Of course she was home. Where else would she be?"

Flossie wriggles out of my arms to the ground.

Flossie stands on one foot and shakes the other leg then switches, pointing her toes, suddenly perky. "Are we going in?"

I walk up to the front porch, stepping carefully around a blue-green area rug folded in half like an omelet, and knock on the doorframe beside the door.

No answer. After the long, silent walk, knocking a second time seems risky, so I just grab Flossie's hand and step through the door frame into the house.

No one's home. At least, that's what it looks like. A set of curtains hangs cockeyed from one nail, the splayed legs of a flattened coffee table take up most of the living room. There is a bookshelf face down with a triangle of squashed pages sticking out from one corner.

The house is so full of wreckage that it takes a lot of looking before I notice her at all.

Kendra, even smaller, more bent and fragile than I had remembered, is sitting absolutely still in a rocking chair in the far corner of the room.

Her eyes are on us but her face shows nothing. Not recognition, not surprise, not fear. Her eyes are marbled, filled with a cloudy blue. I remember Dad saying she can't see much, but the way she is so focused, I know she's watching us as best she can.

"I'm Jay Everton." I swallow. "My father, Braydon Everton, he knows you."

Kendra begins to rock a little back and forth in the chair, still staring at me. Funny how people who talk too much, like my dad, get to me, but when people say nothing I can't stand that either.

"I'm sorry," I say, waving vaguely around.

Kendra continues to rock. The chair squeaks. If you didn't know what it was, you'd think it was bones creaking. Maybe ghosts.

"Which is it?" Her voice, I had forgotten, booms like a boulder.

"Excuse me?"

"Are you Jay, or are you sorry?"

I don't know if this is supposed to be a joke. For all the times I stopped by here with Dad, I can't remember much about her. Did she have a sense of humor? I guess I never got to know her well. Maybe she was always a little terrifying.

"Both, I guess."

Flossie yawns loudly.

Kendra's cloudy eyes slide back to me. "What do you want?"

"Do you, uh, have any gasoline?" I feel foolish even before the words are out of my mouth.

"Braydon send you?"

I nod.

Kendra laughs. Then, abruptly, stops laughing and frowns like she's tasted something sour. "He's a fool."

She lifts one arm from the wooden armrest and waves it around at the mess surrounding her. "Does it look like I've got gas? They took it all. Everything they could get their hands on." Through the window I can see the smashed jam jars outside. Whoever did this wasn't looking for food to eat or scrap to sell.

She stares hard at me, as if willing me to be afraid. There is something like a fairy tale witch about her face. "They forgot just one thing."

Kendra leans forward and pushes herself to her feet. Once she's up she just stands there for a minute, swaying slightly as she gets balanced, then slides one foot forward and inches toward the doorway. Her slippers push past splintered table legs and scattered papers. I step back, out of her way, and pull Flossie back, too.

When Kendra gets to where the front door was she clamps one hand on either side of the doorframe and stands there, bracing herself.

Flossie tugs on my hand and I lean down so she can whisper. "What was it they forgot?"

I shake my head. I don't know.

Kendra stands in the doorway for a long time without saying anything. Then she leans back, opens her mouth wide, and bellows. "You wrecked my home. You destroyed my supplies. Now come on back, Phoenix, and finish the job!"

After that, the silence is loud. Is it possible to hear other people listening? I picture every black-clad Phoenix in the city turning their heads in unison toward the little house where Kendra, Flossie and I stand in the doorway.

"You forgot *me*!" Kendra says. Her voice breaks and at the same time she heaves forward and loses her grip on the doorframe. I jump to grab her. I stick my head under her shoulder and she leans against me, heavier than I would have thought, and I help her turn around. Up close she smells like autumn leaves. Flossie drops to the floor and pushes away the broken table legs to clear a path.

It isn't until Kendra is back in her chair that I remember to breathe again.

I don't know what to say then, except I think repeating *I'm sorry* a second time would not help. So instead, I slip the backpack off my shoulders, drop to my knees, set the bag on the floor, unzip it and take out the smoked salmon. I step forward, hold it out to her like an offering. She takes it, and I step back. Flossie and I watch while she unwraps it, carefully pressing closed bag after bag and setting them on her lap.

Then she looks up at me and nods once, curtly, without smiling, as if we have given her exactly what she expected to receive. She pinches a flake of fish off in her fingers and slips it between her thin lips. She closes her eyes, swallows, rocks for a bit.

Flossie and I just stand there, watching her.

She takes a sip of water from a jar on the windowsill beside her and sets it down. "They took my gas. I had a five-gallon container, full."

"Do you know where we could get some?"

Kendra shakes her head. "I don't know anything for sure anymore. Except that if a person doesn't eat she will die, and I expect I would have gotten there sooner or later if you hadn't come along and brought me this, so thank you."

"It's no big deal," I shrug. The fish reminds me of something I had wanted to ask about. "It was smoked by someone who knows you. His name's Andrew. He used to--I mean, he *says* he used to live next door to you. Then his brother was kidnapped, and his mom went off looking for him, and he was eating weeds in his backyard until you spotted him and sent him to the Key Peninsula. He still lives there now with my grandma, Jody Everton, and a few other people. You saved his life. He told me."

Kendra shakes her head. "No. Nope. You've been misled."

"You don't remember him?"

"Sure I remember Andrew. Cute little boy, always toddling around after his older brother, older brother always pushing him away. I remember he was left behind. He was in the yard putting dandelions in his mouth, I remember that." Kendra nods, remembering. "It's true I helped get him out to the Key Peninsula. But that part about his brother being kidnapped and his mom going off to look for him, that part's a lie."

"His brother never left?"

"Patrick left all right, but he left of his own accord. Just walked off one day, fifteen-years-old and never came home again. Joined up with the Phoenix." Kendra wags a hand in the air. "Everybody knew."

"His mother knew?"

"The whole neighborhood knew."

"But that doesn't make sense. Andrew remembers going with his mom to the high school and trying to get the secretary to tell them where Patrick went after school."

"The school secretary doesn't keep track of things like that."

"But the fact that his mom asked proves she didn't know where he was, right?"

Kendra shakes her head. "She might not have known exactly where he went, but she knew why, and she knew he could get himself back home whenever he wanted. Her taking off after him though, I never got that. They say she went crazy. I figured she joined the Phoenix herself. Join 'em if you can't beat 'em sort of thing." Kendra rocks back and forth. "The dad took off years before. No money coming in. She was gonna lose the house."

"So they never went around the high school banging on doors trying to get someone to talk to them about Patrick?"

"Did he say that?" She laughs once, like a cough. "Think about it. How would a person remember something like that from way back when he was only four years old?"

"He remembered the part about eating weeds right, and you giving him a bath and food and sending him on the ferry to live at Grandma's."

"Only because I wrote all that down in a letter I sent with him to Jody. She must have told him, and now he's gone and imagined a memory for himself. Poor kid. I'm sure he's lonely."

"He says he's got friends in Tacoma. He visits all the time."

"Does he?" Kendra's eyebrows rise. "How does he get here?"

"I think one of his friends has a boat?"

"And how did he meet that friend? And why does the friend need a boat? Did you ask him?"

I shake my head.

Kendra frowns. "I don't know Andrew anymore, but it was his brother Patrick and a couple of other thugs who came here last night and destroyed my house." She pauses, rocking. "It might have been a minute, but I would know Patrick anywhere. In April, Patrick and his friends went next door to what used to be his house and terrorized the family living there now. To the point they packed up and disappeared. Then they try to set up a Phoenix headquarters right next door! I guess what I do is so well-known there's no real point for me to go on doing it. That's what I was thinking about when you showed up. Just sitting here, wondering how long it would take me to die."

Kendra sighs and turns to the window. "You asked about gas," she says after a while. "The only people that may have any are not people you want to be dealing with."

"Phoenix?"

Kendra nods.

"I figured. Where?"

"You'll have to pretend you are just fine with how they're destroying our city."

"I can do that."

"Don't tell them your name. Do not. If they hear the name *Everton* no one's making it out alive."

Flossie, gasping, claps a hand over her mouth.

"I know."

"And no guarantees they still have gas at all." Kendra pauses. "You ever been to the mall?"

Chapter Fourteen: Run!

The Tacoma Mall is all the way on the south side of Tacoma, close to Steilacoom, but Before, that wasn't so far away. Families would go there in their cars and park in a gigantic parking lot that circles the mall and backs up to I-5. No matter what neighborhood you lived in it took no more than ten minutes to get to the mall. The city planned it like that. Maybe it was a law?

I always had a picture of the Tacoma Mall in my mind from stories I've heard, even though I'd never seen it in real life. It is filled with stores, buildings inside a building, lined up in long hallways going off in every direction. Hundreds of stores, maybe a thousand, and each one selling something different. Music, jewelry, shoes, hair ties, underwear, candy, toys, books, tiny charms and erasers and notebooks, video games, music, and movies. All sorts of stuff people might have wanted but did not actually *need*.

All sorts of food, too, not groceries to take home, but food that had already been cooked and was still hot and meant to be eaten right there on the spot where it was purchased. They served it on plates made out of styrofoam, the same stuff they'd put under docks so they float, and gave away free forks and spoons made out of plastic, just like Quick Stop used to give away plastic cups and straws.

Back Before, going to the mall was a great way to spend a day. Teenagers met there and wandered around, buying stuff, eating food with plastic forks, playing games on their cell phones. They only had one giant mall for the whole city, but it was enough.

We walk. I give up carrying Flossie--she slows me down--and let her run loops behind and ahead like a normal kid. I think about Sarah again. It's funny all the things I can't remember. I don't know the date of Martin Luther King's *I Have a Dream* speech. I got all screwed up in math when the teacher had us dividing fractions, and that was just a review from last year.

Even so, right now I can picture exactly the way Sarah tosses her head. I can see it just like it's happening inside my mind. I know the way her long blond hair flops over one shoulder like a waterfall. And the way she laughs. I can hear it.

We are out of Kendra's neighborhood and onto the freeway overpass. The scale is off. Either the world is too big or we're too small. The freeway is a very wide road, and walking it feels like touring the ruins of some ancient civilization.

What gets me is the dashed yellow lines dividing the road into three lanes. Each dash is probably ten feet long. In between the dashes there is a blank space that's probably eight or ten feet long too. Mom said that from a fast-moving car they look like a light flashing on and off, and drivers knew that meant it was okay to change lanes and move past another car.

Because once upon a time people moved so fast a ten-foot yellow line looked like a flashing light.

Because once upon a time there were so many cars sometimes they needed to pass.

We leave the overpass at the 56th Street exit, like Kendra said, down a long hill, then left. The houses are smaller here, one-story for the most part, scotch broom and blackberries filling in the yards, none of the wide front porches and flower beds and other nice little things that the houses in our neighborhood have. Funny that I don't notice those things when I see them, but I do notice when they're gone.

There are more fences around the yards here, not wood fences to keep raccoons out, but tall chain link fences with loops of razor wire on top.

I'm thinking about fences when Flossie stops running loops and squeezes my hand. She's spotted someone.

I keep walking.

Flossie squeezes again, harder this time. Squeezes and squeezes.

"I know. Stop," I whisper. "Just stop. I'm trying to think."

Flossie stops squeezing but holds very tight to my hand. We walk for another minute and then I see a place to hide.

I turn and look. I stop walking and make it really obvious that I can see him walking behind us. He's close enough now I can hear his boots scraping the pavement anyway so there's no reason I wouldn't naturally turn around. He looks like the guy Dad and I saw this morning, a little wider maybe, but dressed all in black, with a black cloth over his nose and mouth so you can't really make out what he looks like.

He stops walking, too, when he sees me looking, stops and gives a little wave, hand under his chin, fingers waggling. I can't see his mouth under that black cloth but I can picture it, a Jack-o-Lantern smile, holes where teeth fell out. He's about one block back now, maybe a little more. I have no idea how far back he was when Flossie first spotted him, or how fast he's catching up.

I snap my head back around and yank Flossie left onto the next block. The house on the corner has been looted. There's no door at all, and from the street you can see a coat rack with a sweater still hanging up on it inside. Real quick, I shove open the gate. It bumps against the cement walkway and jams so I have to turn sideways and squeeze in. Then, instead of going inside the house, I jump over an upholstered kitchen chair, sort of half-falling across it, then up again and over a splintered wooden cabinet and a pile of papers, then down behind the cabinet in the tall dry grass, pulling Flossie down behind me. She lands on top of me, hard, grunting directly into my nostrils.

I wrap my arm over her back. "Don't move."

We lie pressed together for the longest minute of my life. Breathing is tough. Flossie's hair flutters up and down on my face. Slow footsteps get closer on the sidewalk. I don't know if the grass covers us completely. I am thinking about a million things all at once. I am thinking about what I will tell Flossie next time she tries to get me to play hide-and-seek with her. *I am never playing hide-and-seek again*, I will say.

I am so ready to jump up and explode, fists flying, that it's almost a surprise when the footsteps move onto the porch. There is the scratch of broken glass underneath his boots, then the sound changes and I know we've tricked him. He's inside.

It's an old Craftsman-style house, like the one we live in, only smaller. One thing I know about Craftsman homes is as soon as you go in the front door you can choose to go up the staircase or stay on the main floor. There is a pause and I hear him go up the stairs, the sound of his feet on the riders, each step a hollow thump one half-note above the last.

It's a familiar sound, and I feel oddly sentimental all of a sudden. There have been times at our house that I sat on the front lawn hearing Flossie, running inside to kiss Mom, pee, or grab Zebra before we walked to school.

As soon as I hear him on the second floor I push Flossie off me, hoist her to her feet and scramble over the cabinet that hid us. Flossie falls. It hasn't rained and the papers aren't waterlogged yet. I pull her to her feet again and sort of drag her over the cabinet and the upholstered chair, through the narrow gate, out to the sidewalk and back the way we came.

I don't have to tell her to run. We just do. We run.

We run fast. Me in front and Flossie behind, back along the block where we had been walking.

We don't wait. We don't look back. We run and run.

The whole world is silent except for the thump of our boots on the ground. Our breath.

And my heart.

Chapter Fifteen: Flossie Finds a Way

All the doors to the Tacoma Mall are locked. I should have known they would be. Rusty chains and rusty padlocks. The glass is nailed over with old gray boards. This is no rush job either, like our house, but solid wood, thick boards and plenty of long nails. *No Admittance -- City of Tacoma* has been stenciled in tall blue letters.

Flossie and I walk all the way around the enormous building trying to find the way in. That takes the better part of an hour, and in the end we're right back where we started.

I drop down on a curb, pull out my water canteen and take a long drink. I feel woozy, dried up, too tired to be upset. I push my pant legs up to my knees and work my fingers into my sore calves.

At least we don't have to worry about anyone sneaking up on us here. The parking lot is bigger than anything I've ever seen, a parking lot ocean. I can see why the Phoenix like it here. You'd have to walk up to a person for a full five minutes before you reached them.

From where I'm sitting I can see what must be the highway they call I-5. Everyone who was around Before calls it one road, but I see that I-5 is actually two roads, two long parallel roads, most likely one for going north and one for going south. I left the compass on the boat so I don't know which way is which. Doesn't matter. People have blocked the roads with all sorts of garbage, washing machines, gutted-out cars, a refrigerator, machine parts I don't recognize, even an old race boat, covered in graffiti.

Flossie seems energized by the walk, as if getting out of the dark house with our worrywart parents was exactly what she needed. She hops up and down on the curb, one foot than the other, humming. Her ponytail bounces.

"Jay," she says after a minute, "I have to pee."

"Go behind that bush right there."

"Behind that bush right *there*?" Flossie looks at me as if I've ordered her to tap dance on the Monopoly box.

"Do you have to go or don't you?"

"Okay," she says slowly. "But don't look."

I'm already not looking, so her comment doesn't require a response. I shade my eyes with my hand and squint toward the horizon. "Jay, there's something back here you really have to see," Flossie calls.

Most of the time when she's found something I *really have to see,* it turns out to be a caterpillar with a yellow stripe. A colony of ants. Or a rock that looks like a heart, a little bit, if you hold it a certain way.

"Jay? Did you hear me? You have to see what I found."

"Bring it here," I say. "My legs are sore."

"I can't." There is a pause. "It isn't something I can pick up."

I push down one pant leg and then the other. When I stand up the place on my back between my shoulder blades hurts, from the backpack, also my lower back hurts, and I groan and feel like Kendra.

What if there is no gas?

"You better have your pants zipped up already."

"Of course I do," Flossie says.

I push the branches aside.

"Look." She's pointing to a rectangular vent, about one foot high by two feet wide, the same kind that is bolted into the cement walls at school. It's popped forward a little, with four empty holes where the bolts used to be. "Does that look weird to you?"

I kneel down next to the vent. The vertical parts of the metal frame are a half inch separate from the cement wall, barely hanging on. I stick a finger in on either side and the vent falls out onto the ground. I stick my head in and I can see a large, dark, empty room. Cool air flows out like an invitation.

It'll be a squeeze, but we can fit.

"Flossie," I sit up and pat her head like a puppy. "You're a genius."

"Oh no," Flossie shakes her head from side to side, eyes wide, face serious. "We can't go in."

"Why not?"

"There are signs."

I laugh. "What did you think we were doing sitting around here then?"

Flossie shrugs, focused on something imaginary just beyond my shoulder. She's hurt that I laughed at her, I can tell. "Taking a break before walking back home, I guess?"

"Flossie," I say, then sigh and say nothing for a minute because I don't know the words to use to tell her what I have to say. "Those signs don't matter anymore. None of the old rules matter. Even the City of Tacoma doesn't exist, not like it used to. Look," I point at a *No Admittance* sign on the wall a few yards away. "It says for more information go to their website."

"What's a website?"

"A computer thing from Before. Proof those signs don't matter. And we aren't going home again. It's too dangerous, you know that. Mom and Dad need us to go stay with Grandma for a while. It's a nice place and you'll like it." I don't mention Andrew. I don't know what to say about Andrew.

There is silence.

"It isn't a choice, okay? Thing is, we need gas to get there. Dad thought Kendra had some, but she didn't, so she sent us here, where she thinks there might be some. If we can get inside, we can find some. Later, when things settle down, Mom and Dad will find a way for us all to be together again." I try to think about what our parents would say. "It's for the best."

Flossie picks a leaf off the bush, shreds it with a thumbnail and lets the pieces fall like confetti. "We aren't going home?"

I shake my head. "No."

"Not ever?"

"Not for a very long time."

She stares at the bush, frowning hard, like she does just before yelling that something isn't fair. This is the face she made when Mom told her stealing cheese samples means she can't go to the farmer's market anymore.

We're more alike than different, Flossie and I. One day we will both be adults facing the same problems in the same world, and when that day comes there will be no more patting her on the head like a puppy. We're partners in the future world. I've never thought about her growing up before. She was something for the three of us, myself and our parents, to deal with, something to take care of. We help her do stuff she's too little to do herself, we read to her, play with her, make sure she's eating, make sure she's happy, make sure she's safe.

"So no more school? No more running away from kidnappers?"

"No more school. No more kidnappers."

Flossie grins, surprising me. And then she drops down and wriggles inside the vent.

***

Two summers ago, in August, one of Dad's teacher friends at the community college drowned, and our whole family walked almost four hours to the church where they had his funeral. I had never even met him, and so the whole way there I was feeling grouchy and thinking the funeral was a real waste of time, especially since Chase Messerman had asked me to help him build a fort.

But once we were there, out of the sun, inside the cool cavern of the church, a small part of me enjoyed the experience. I had never been to church before, and I spent the whole funeral staring up at the ceiling, my eyes running along the long, thick wooden beams over our heads, playing freeze tag with Chase in my mind.

It is huge and cool and dark, like that church, inside the mall. Flossie and I walk through an enormous hallway toward the light, where more of the same enormous hallways come together in perpendicular corners and the roof rises up another hundred or so feet.

Flossie sucks in her breath. We stare. There are glass windows on the ceiling, instead of regular wood, which is lucky because otherwise there'd be no light at all. I wonder why other buildings all have roofs made of wood, if glass does the same thing but lets the light through, too.

The glass is green, painted with the slime of winter rain. There's a thick branch which must have blown down in a storm. The bottom of each pane is webbed with black leaves, rotten pine cones, and black muck.

Before, it was probably someone's job to clean those windows on a regular basis. They would have had to wipe away the slime and scoop the dead leaves and toss the branches off the glass all the time. I think Birdman would have been good at that job. I would, too. I would like to have a bird's eye view of everyone walking around inside the mall, see them without them seeing me.

Now it's only a matter of time before nature piles so much dirt and branches up there that the windows break open and it all falls through. Then the rain will get in, then birds, which means seeds and plants. The Ancient Tacoma Ruins. That's what they'll call the mall one day.

Flossie and I stand there looking up.

"The people who lived Before must have been very tall."

"That's not true," I say. "Mom and Dad lived Before, and they aren't any taller than normal. People just like building things big." I think about the blanket forts I build for Flossie sometimes. She's always begging me to bring in another sheet from the closet.

"How come?"

"How do I know? Being inside something big makes people feel important, I guess."

"It makes *some* people feel like breaking things, apparently," Flossie says, frowning at an overturned planter and a pile of half-burnt wood where someone once--who knows how many months or years ago--built a campfire.

I get a creepy feeling then. Maybe just left over from our close call earlier, but my skin prickles like someone's watching, so I grab Flossie's hand and pull her across the hallway. "Let's find that gas."

Then Flossie and I walk up and down every single enormous hallway in the whole enormous mall.

The stores--there must be a hundred--line each wall like dark holes where teeth used to be. Every single one of them has a metal grate across it that wiggles back and forth a bit but is locked tight--up, down and sideways--when I yank them. And I yank them all.

Inside the stores it's hard to make out much, but they look empty. There's a few cardboard boxes here and there, and a few still have metal racks where clothes or sneakers or candy used to be displayed.

About halfway down the final hallway we come across a mystery. A large, red, pickup truck.

"Who parks *inside* the mall?" Flossie sticks her fingers into the latticework on the truck's silvery front grate.

I shake my head. "There's a price sticker. It was for sale. Maybe it was the last truck they ever made before gas prices went up." I cup my hands and press my face against the truck window, but it's dark glass and I can't see.

"The very last one, you think? And it's been sitting here ever since? Waiting for someone to walk in and buy it?"

"Probably."

"And now that no one comes here, no one is ever going to?"

"Nope. Right. You got it." My skin starts to prickle and I do a 360 on my heels, just to be sure. I'd rather keep moving.

Flossie frowns. "That's sad!"

"Poor truck. Poor, never-going-to-be-driven truck. Now let's go."

I look at Flossie. She's silent, rubbing her palms alongside the cab door like she's in love with it.

"Help me."

Flossie shakes her head.

"Yell or something. Look around. Get your hands off that dumb truck."

Flossie presses her chest to the truck like it's magnetic. "No thank you. I choose not to yell. You shouldn't either. Why would I yell for my kidnappers?" She shakes her head. "You heard Kendra. If they hear the name *Everton* we're done for."

"Shush!"

I sigh, turn, and yell for gas. Flossie starts yapping like a terrier every time I open my mouth, loud as she can, covering me up.

"Act like a human being," I say, but she's impossible to argue with.

After a while I figure if someone was going to respond they would have, so I grab Flossie's hand and pull her away from the truck.

We are walking past a big store at the end of the third hall when Flossie lets out a scream.

I whip around to see what she's caught sight of. In the window are three mannequins in a row, all of them naked, all of them bald, the last one without a head.

"Not real," I try to sound cheerful, remembering what Mom said about mannequins. "They're giant dolls. Before, workers would put clothes on them so people knew what the clothes would look like on themselves."

Each of the mannequins is posed in a different way. The one on the left has her hand at her shoulder palm up like she is holding a small tray or something. The headless one is against the wall.

Flossie wipes her nose on my shirt. "I hate Before."

Once we've walked every hallway, Fossie and I sit down on a flat stone bench in the center in the greenish underwater light. "We could live here. This bench could be our bed. Night-night," Flossie says, lying down on her belly, closing her eyes and pressing her face against the cool stone, first one cheek and then the other. I take off the backpack and unzip it so we can eat dinner.

Water first. Flossie sits up, grabs the canteen and chugs greedily until I take it away from her. The carrots are wrapped neatly in creased brown paper. I unfold the paper and smooth it with my hands so it makes a sort of placemat.

The eggs are still in the cloth like I wrapped them in at Grandma's house. I never noticed how pretty they look in all the different colors and patterns. Brown. White. Blue-green. Speckled. The two of us sit cross-legged with the food between us. Flossie rolls an egg on the bench to break the shell, picks off the first few pieces then slides the rest off with her thumb.

I take a long drink of water. My eyes are resting on the colorful eggs when I hear it. A monster-size match being scraped against stone. A mechanical roar. I know what that sound is. All the way on the other side of the mall, the truck engine is starting up.

Flossie, her mouth full of egg, looks at me with wide eyes. I can't see the truck yet, but I can hear it accelerating.

I grab Flossie's arm and we jump up to run. But where? We're trapped. All the stores are locked up tight, and it occurs to me I have absolutely no idea where to find the vent we came in.

There is a short hallway leading to a set of glass doors, and I run there, like a fly to a window, and shake the handles so hard the chains on the outside clang.

I spin around. The door handle cuts into my back, hard. Flossie's twenty feet away, squatting behind another enormous flowerpot. She's got both of her hands out for me. I shake my head. She's screaming something, but her words are eaten up by the noise, or my panic, or both.

Then the truck, fast as a meteor, appears down the hall and peels a full circle around the center atrium, just inches from the bench where Flossie and I had just been peeling hard boiled eggs.

I see a hand gripping the steering wheel, a shirt sleeve, nothing else. I do know whoever is driving doesn't have much experience. In the hands of a driver with experience, an engine hums like a happy beehive. This one squeals.

The truck loops the center bench two, three times. Then, the front end clips the corner and sends the truck ricocheting down the short hallway toward Flossie and me. Flossie jumps to her feet and leaps onto the metal grate covering the nearest storefront, like a cat escaping dogs. She's three feet above my head before I can move.

The truck skids to a stop in front of me, laying streaky black tracks on the floor. The way it stops, the driver's side door is jammed against the wall, so the driver can't get out except through the other side. There's a crunch of metal then a hiss. I hear the door bang the flowerpot, trying to open.

Then, as if from a still pool in the center of a fast river, I notice a person standing behind me, and I hear a yell.

For a second it's like before, the sound loses its way before reaching my ears, only this time it comes through finally and I understand. "Here," she's yelling. "Over here." She wants to help us.

I look, and I think this really must be the end. I've lost it. I've knocked out. I'm unconscious. I'm having a dream. I'm hallucinating. All the stress, the walking, the sun, the heat, all the things I have come to learn in the past week has bubbled my blood and made me crazy.

Because out of all the people in the entire city, all the people in the entire world who could be there ready to help, the person who is there is Sarah.

Chapter Sixteen: Into the Dumpster

Flossie and I follow Sarah down the windowless hallway toward a door. I make out the word *Management* before she slams it open. Hadn't I seen this door before? Didn't I try them all?

I can't think. I slip through with Flossie behind me, fast as a whip. We dash through a small room, through another door, and we're outside. Sarah shoves the door closed and locks it behind us.

I bend over, hands on my knees, gasping like a fish. Flossie, beside me, does the same. There's an ancient picnic table chained to the ground and next to it a cement enclosure, tall and square with wide wooden doors on one side. I remember seeing it earlier, when we were trying to find a way into the mall. Flossie had asked me what it was, and I told her it was where they locked up kids who asked too many questions.

Sarah works a key on the padlock. Out of nowhere, she laughs. "You really shook those doors," she exhales. "I thought it was the ghost of Christmas past."

"Sorry," I say.

"No apology needed." She shakes her head. The padlock opens. She pulls back the door and waves us inside. She closes it behind us, locks it by sticking her hand through a loose board, then jiggles the board back into place. "Home sweet home."

It's a Dumpster. A metal box people Before used to store trash on its way to the landfill. But why did people used to lock up trash?

"You live *here*?" Flossie's voice is quiet.

"I have it fixed up real nice. Want to see?"

Flossie nods, and Sarah loops her fingers together and bends down to make Flossie a step. There is the clang of sheet metal as Flossie's boots land inside.

"Wow," she says. "You've got to see this, Jay."

Sarah tilts her head toward one shoulder and her eyes narrow a bit. "Jay?" she says. "That sounds familiar."

"You, too." I wipe the sweat off my forehead, wondering what to do if she asks about my last name. "I mean, you look familiar. Do you go to Pierce?" I used to spend forty minutes a day gazing at the tiny breakaway filaments of her hair underneath the fluorescent lights. Of course I don't say that. "I think we have a class together?"

"Fourth period. Washington State History." She looks me up and down like I'm a strange piece of art. "You've been absent."

214

"Visiting relatives." I would like to know if she noticed I was absent, or if Mrs. Markus said something. "Did I miss anything?"

She shrugs. "I guess it doesn't matter now."

"I guess not." I want to ask about how she spotted us inside, how she opened the Management door, and if she knows where to find gas, but I can't because all of a sudden I don't know what to do with my hands. I hook my thumbs through my pants pockets, then decide that looks dumb, so I put them on my hips, like our gym teacher. Then I drop them to my sides and stare at my boots.

"My name is Sarah."

I nod politely. "Jay."

"I know already, remember?" She laughs her musical little laugh. From inside the Dumpster Flossie is humming. Sarah tilts her head. "Want to see?"

"Sure," I gesture for her to go first, mostly to look chivalrous, but also because I don't want her staring at my rear as I flail around trying to maneuver myself through the opening, which is at least three feet off the ground.

Inside, the Dumpster's set up pretty close to a regular kid's bedroom. There's a small table. A jar on the table with seashells and tiny starfish. There's Sarah's backpack, unzipped and overflowing, the army jacket and a hairbrush on top. There is also a cot mattress, with a plaid sleeping bag laid out on top of it.

Flossie has made herself comfortable on Sarah's bed, leaning against the wall with her arms folded behind, boots off, legs crossed. "I love what you've done with this place," she says

"Thank you!"

I don't want to be the only one standing, so I sit on the other side of the little table. I tuck my boots under my knees, scraping loudly across the metal floor. "So," I clear my throat, "what was all that about in there?"

"Someone has it in for you."

"Who?"

"Shouldn't I be asking you that?" Sarah laughs and settles back against the wall. "How'd you get inside the mall anyway? Probably just some nutcase. I'm sure Junior heard the commotion. He'll be here soon. He'll know."

"Who is Junior? Why is he coming here?" Flossie's probably hoping Junior is a kid her age.

"Junior's my boyfriend. I mean--" Sarah pauses and lowers her chin in a shy grin. "We don't use that word. But he'll come check on me."

"Does he live here, too?" Flossie looks around.

"He lives at Tent City, but he's at the mall during the day. He helps me and brings me food and stuff when he can. He's the one who gave me these keys." Sarah wags her keychain.

Flossie leans forward. "What's he do at the mall?"

"He sells gas with the other guys. They're out at the tire shop on the far side of the parking lot."

"We came here looking for gas!" Flossie's face settles. "So, your boyfriend's a Phoenix then." My sister is good at taking pieces of information and putting them together like a jigsaw puzzle. However, she hasn't made the connection that the person who kidnapped her and the Grand Order of Phoenix are one and the same. She pinches her nose with her fingers. "Phoenix stink."

Sarah laughs and picks up the hairbrush.

"How'd you and Junior meet?"

"You really want to know?" Sarah lays her long hair over one shoulder and begins brushing. Maybe she'll inspire Flossie. "It started with my stepdad, Bryce. Do you remember that first morning when the president was shot? What was it, a Sunday?"

I nod. It feels like a century.

"Well, I was sleeping. It must have been about six-thirty? I wake up to gunshots. *Bam bam bam!* Real fast. And, like two feet away from me. I don't know if you know how loud a rifle is?" Sarah keeps brushing without waiting for an answer. "It's loud."

"My step dad, he's kind of obsessed with following the news. He heard about the president, and the next thing you know he's put his hunting rifle together and is firing rounds into the sky." She shakes her head. "Summoning his own little imaginary army."

"Must be a morning person."

"That's hilarious," Sarah frowns. "More like a midnight person. He was still drunk from the day before." She's finished brushing her hair and now walks her fingers across her head, separating it into three parts like Mom does for Flossie's braid.

I look up. Three feet above my head a plastic lid forms a roof. There's a bend in it that lets in the light. The way the sun is right now makes a tiny spotlight on the metal behind Sarah's head.

"Anyway, long story short, Mom decides that's as good a reason as any to start drinking alongside Bryce again. And I know how that goes, so I left."

"That was it? You've lived here ever since?"

"Not at first. First I tried Tent City. They let anybody stay."

I nod, happy to be able to add something to the story. "They were burning tires when I went by."

"They've been doing that for days. They're trying to send smoke signals, call people to meet." She shrugs. "I'm like, what do you have against tires? You can build stuff with tires."

"Right! That's what I thought, too."

"But I went there anyway, and found a nice quiet spot way off from the fires, and pitched my tent. I'd planned ahead and packed Bryce's size 12 boots to set outside of the tent, like a decoy, you know?

"So I hadn't been there for even a day when I was walking down the road, and two huge Phoenix guys come up behind me. They were making jokes, yelling things, and when I turned around they both had baseball bats and they were holding them up like this," Sarah puts her fists to her shoulder like she's waiting for a pitch.

"I ignored them. Just kept walking. They started saying things and laughing. I knew I shouldn't but I got scared and ran. And that's how we met. I ran straight into Junior. I could tell he was a Phoenix too--dressed in black--but he yelled at them and they disappeared. That's it." Sarah smiles at Flossie. "What do you think? Romantic?"

Flossie stops tying knots in the drawstring of Sarah's sleeping bag and looks up. "So you're a Phoenix, too?"

"Do I look like a Phoenix?" Sarah grabs the red striped shirt she's wearing and looks down at it. "What's your story? How did the two of you wind up all the way on the other side of town?"

Flossie's starts talking before I can even think. "We're going to live with our grandmother on the

Key Peninsula." She shifts around on the mattress to face Sarah squarely. "Our parents are sending us. It's not because they don't love us, but because it's too dangerous for us at home."

Sarah nods and spins the hairbrush on the little glass table. A single motion sets it spinning like a top, like it could keep on spinning for infinity unless something else came along to stop it. After a while Sarah sighs. "It is the Collectivists' fault, you know."

"Their fault for what?" I ask.

"That the president's dead! They are the ones who've been complaining for years about everything he does to help our country. It was one of them who came up with the plan to kill him. It was one of them who pulled the trigger. They want to take over."

The Dumpster feels stuffy, like all the air has been breathed already. "How do you know that?"

"It's all Junior talks about." Sarah spins the hairbrush.

"But how do you know for sure?"

Sarah doesn't answer, and the question hangs awkwardly between us. But how does she know for sure that a Collectivist that killed McAllister? How does anyone know anything for sure? The radio, the teacher, the textbook, a boyfriend, a kid's own mom and dad--They all have their own way of looking at things. They all have their own sources they trust, and those sources have sources, and so on. I watch the hairbrush spin. I wasn't in the room when President McAllister was shot. Therefore, I will never know for sure who is responsible for his death.

I wonder if Flossie already knew that the president was killed, or if hearing this is scaring her. She has her back to us, so I can't tell.

"Don't you think they--" I shake my head and start again. "What if the Collectivists have good ideas about how to run the country? Shouldn't we let them try? I mean, it's not like things are going so great now." I gesture vaguely. "Thirteen-year-olds living in Dumpsters."

"I'm fourteen. And it was my choice to live here." Sarah's eyebrows push down in the middle and she scowls. "Some people just grow up fast."

"I believe that everyone wants the best for our country. They might have different ideas about how to do that, but the Collectivists just want to make our country like Before."

"Well, they shouldn't have started by shooting a guy in the stomach." She shakes her head and glances at Flossie, who is still busy tying knots. "And they ought to know the gas isn't coming back."

"They know that. I mean, everyone knows that. But they saw it coming first."

Sarah lowers her chin and looks at me as if over invisible glasses. "It seems like you're making a lot of excuses for the Collectivists."

I lower my chin and glare right back. "It seems like you think you know a lot about something you don't."

Now that I know what Sarah's really like I'm going to miss the way she was in my imagination.

There's a sound from outside. Boots on gravel.

"What took you so long!" Sarah yells, pushing past me.

"Ask about gas!" Flossie says.

Sarah undoes the lock on the wooden door, steps outside and pulls it shut behind her before I can see anything.

Then Flossie stands and pops her head into the bend in the Dumpster's plastic roof like a mole. Two seconds later she drops back down and buries her face in my shirt.

"What happened?" I whisper, patting her back. "What did you see? Was he the one at school?"

Flossie nods.

"Did he see you?"

She shrugs, then shakes her head.

Sarah's face appears beside the Dumpster.

I sit up. "Well, thanks, but we better get going. It's gonna get dark."

Flossie cups her hand and whispers in my ear. "We can't leave her with him!"

Sarah waves as if she doesn't care what we do, swings gracefully inside and settles down cross legged.

Flossie shakes her head, looking serious. "I don't like it." Then Flossie turns to Sarah, up on her feet like it's a formal announcement. "That guy--" She points, "the one you call your *boyfriend*, he's the one who tried to kidnap me at school. He's the one who has been trying to kidnap me for years."

I hook a finger through one of Flossie's belt loops and drop her onto my lap. The sudden weight of her reverbates up the Dumpster walls.

"He's been trying to kidnap me all my life!"

"What?" Sarah tilts her head as if Flossie's speaking gibberish. "Kidnap? No, not Junior. You're wrong. He has a little brother who looks like him. Junior would never hurt anyone."

"If he's a Phoenix he would. There's no saying what a Phoenix would and would not do. How long have you known him for anyway? A week?"

Sarah shakes her head the whole time I am talking. "No, he's a good one. He saved me from a gang of Phoenix!"

I laugh. "You ran. You saw baseball bats and then ran. Then Junior just *happened* to be there and just *happened* to see it and decided to protect some kid he didn't know?" I laugh once. "You got set up."

Sarah stares like she's wrapping her mind around something she never thought about before.

"Let's go Flossie," I push her off my lap, and we go.

Chapter Seventeen:
When Gas Catches Fire

We start off walking toward the marina, but after a few hundred feet I take a left and sit down in the shade behind an old building to think, Flossie follows. I can't just stroll up to Junior and ask for gas. If he wanted to sell it to me, he would have. But I can't walk to the marina without gas. It's too far, and there's no point. I'd just have to walk back here tomorrow.

"Hot now," Flossie says.

"It's been hot all day."

"No," she points. "That's what the sign says."

I turn. Behind me, in the window, there's an old sign with clear glass letters. It does say *Hot Now*.

I'm not in the mood to contemplate weird remnants of Before. If Junior won't sell me gas, I'll have to steal it. Knowing where they sell it helps. But I don't know my way around the tire shop. I don't know where in the tire shop the gas is kept. I don't know if it's locked. I don't know how many people are there. I don't know if they have weapons.

The tire shop backs up to a sort of ridge, with a dozen or so houses behind. I could walk around the long way, go down the street and get into the backyard of one of those houses. From there I could watch the tire place from behind. I could figure out where the gas is kept, then when no one's looking, go in. Maybe I should take a night just to watch. Go just after dawn, when it's quiet.

That's what I will do. I make up my mind. Watch and wait and let them forget we were ever here.

With my plan settled, I set my hands behind me and lean back against the pebbly concrete wall, closing my eyes to the sun. I breathe deep and feel almost good. Flossie is using the curb as a balance beam, hopping and swooping and humming to herself. The sun is low, silhouetting her. My mind wanders over the details of the new plan.

But then, from across the parking lot, I hear Sarah unlocking the door outside the Dumpster and see her start walking. She's bent forward, like she's upset. Sarah walks around the side of the mall. It isn't hard to figure out where she's headed.

Then I know what I have to do. I run. The instant Sarah disappears I'm sprinting as fast as I can go. Flossie is running, too. I don't even have to tell her. I hear her boots hitting the ground. We round the far side of the mall, opposite from Sarah.

I have to make it to the tire shop before she does, use the sixty seconds it takes her to tell Junior about us to sneak in, grab the gas, and go.

Flossie catches up, comes close to passing me. I have to grab onto the back of her shirt to stop her when we get to the second corner, just yards from the tire shop. I am too out of breath to speak but grabbing her shirt works. Flossie stumbles, then stops. She puts her hands on her knees and pants heavily at the grass. I wipe the sweat off my forehead with the palm of my hand and poke my head around the corner at the tire shop.

It's a box. A single-story box-shaped building with a plain flat front, save for four big garage doors propped half open like sleepy eyes.

Right away I spot Junior. Patrick. Whatever name he's going by now.

He does look like Andrew, but taller and skinnier, black clothes head to foot. He has a bandana tied around his forehead, and sunglasses, big mirror ones, probably from somewhere in the mall. I watch as he stretches, hands on his hips and twisting his shoulders first one way then the other.

The sunglasses make it impossible to see which way he's looking.

I wonder what I should do next. How to make it across the parking lot and get inside. I feel like a mouse contemplating an owl.

Then his head turns. He's looking away from me, toward the other corner of the mall. He hears something. Sarah.

Flossie is sitting cross legged in the grass, still catching her breath. "Stay," I tell her.

Junior takes a few steps, his neck craned forward like there's something she's saying that he isn't quite catching. It's probably a tenth of a mile between me and the tire shop. Less than the length of a city block. Less than Grandma's driveway. But there's no scotch broom, no big bushes, nothing at all to hide behind, so it feels huge.

I run. Slip in under one of the big garage doors. I take a breath and duck into the shady front room of the tire shop.

It takes my eyes a second to adjust to the dim light, but there's nothing. I am in a large room. A large, empty room. There is absolutely nothing in it as far as I can see. There is a long counter where the cash register must have been, and behind it nothing but dust. To my left there's tall metal shelves that must have stored tires.

I lunge toward the back room. There are more empty shelving units lined up in either direction. I run up and down the aisle, gasping.

There is nothing. No gas. Not even an empty container.

Nothing.

Nothing.

Nothing.

Nothing.

Nothing.

I left my sister within reach of a kidnapper seeking gas that doesn't exist.

There's one more door. I throw it open so hard it bounces back and smacks me in the face. Restroom. Just big enough for one toilet and one sink. Underneath the sink is a cabinet. I throw open both cabinet doors. A cardboard box, creased and greasy and big enough to take up most of the inside. I yank on it. The cardboard tears along the divider bar and I see two old gallon jugs with something sloshing inside.

Gas.

I grab both gallons by the handles, jump to my feet and run through the back exit and outside. There is the ridge, the row of backyards, a bit farther away than I had imagined, but still a good cover. I start left.

A head pops up from behind a scotch broom. Andrew. He steps out. His right hand is tucked behind. "You found the gasoline."

"It was my gas to begin with."

Andrew juts his chin forward. "Took it off your boat myself."

"Then what? You hitched a ride out here? Where did you hide?"

Andrew shrugs. "You never found me because you never thought to look."

"I'll tell Jody. You can never go home again."

Andrew shrugs. "I am home."

Then Andrew pulls his arm out from behind his back and shows me what he has hidden. It's a knife. One of those folding knives with blades that pop in and out. He takes a step toward me, the knife at shoulder height, his hand a fist.

What happens next, it's like my arm doesn't bother getting permission from my brain, it just goes. I shift weight to my left, and with my right arm I heave one gallon of gas up, lean back and swing, hoping to knock him onto the ground.

That's not how it happens though. At the same time I reach up Andrew does too, and when I swing the blade of his knife connects. It cuts deep into the plastic jug and comes out again. Gas is gurgling out onto the pavement and making rivers in the cracks.

Andrew makes another wild swing with the knife, but I stop it this time and the gallon jug knocks the knife out of his hand. He tries to catch it somehow with his other hand, but takes the pointy end of his own knife about halfway between wrist and elbow. He covers it with his hand but right away there is blood coming out from between his fingers, and he looks panicked.

Meanwhile the jug splatters me head to toe before crashing to the ground.

Andrew watches it fall. Just then there is a shout and Junior appears around the corner. Sarah, too. He is sort of half-dragging her, his big palm is clamped over her face. She's clawing at him with both hands.

"Jay *Everton*!" Junior says brightly, as if we are old friends reuniting. "This girl here says you're looking for gas."

Junior passes Sarah off to Andrew with a shove. He grips her tightly, ignoring the blood which now covers his wrist and hand.

"She sure is full of it all of a sudden. Comes racing up from her garbage can telling me I tried to kidnap her new friend's little sister. Wouldn't I remember trying to kidnap someone's little sister? I think she's about ready to sign up with the Collectivists." Junior shakes his head and starts walking toward me. "Jay Everton," he says again. "You're a hard person to track down, you know that?"

I shrug, then hug the remaining gallon of gas to my chest. "Not trying to bother anybody. Just trying to take my gas and get back to the Key Peninsula."

Junior juts his chin toward the gallons in my hands. "What you got is ours, not yours. And I would disagree about you not trying to bother us." Andrew leans forward, pulling Sarah's arm forward too.

He shakes his head like he just doesn't feel up to arguing anymore. He looks me up and down, then he reaches into his pocket and pulls out a matchbox and waves it in front of my face. "You ever wonder what happens when gas catches fire?"

Just then Flossie screams.

I had been so focused on Andrew and Patrick, I hadn't even seen her coming. But it's a good one. Loud enough to split wood. Andrew jerks, losing his grip on Sarah, and right away she dives for the knife. At the same time I turn my shoulder and lunge for Patrick, knocking the matchbox from his hand.

Flossie grabs onto my shirt and holds it tightly. Junior and Andrew both seem smaller, as if losing advantage caused them to shrink.

"Guess I'm in charge of the chickens now?"

***

When we get to the marina I let Flossie and Sarah get in first, then climb in myself and pour the gallon of gas into the tank. I can't help but smile. The smell of the gas on my clothes and in the tank fills my nostrils with a lovely sting. I turn the ignition, grinning like a fool, and putter out of our slip to the place where the marina opens up to the bay.

A minute later I turn the motor off and look down at the deep dark Puget Sound. I think of the giant Pacific octopus, all the way down at the bottom, moving around in the sand.

I clear my throat. "Did you know some of the biggest octopus in the world live right here under the Tacoma Narrows Bridge?"

Sarah is quiet, and I wonder if that was a weird thing to say. "Do they wrap their tentacles around ships and suck them down to the bottom?"

"You're thinking of squid. The octopus who live here are just sort of shy. Shy but smart."

Then Sarah pops up on her knees to look at the water. Gripping the railing, she bends low, almost as low as I did on the way out. She lets go with one hand, sticks it under the water and waves. Sarah is waving to the giant Pacific octopus. "Hello!" she calls cheerfully.

After a minute she straightens up again and smooths back her hair. Her face is red from hanging. She smiles at Flossie, who seems to be deciding whether or not to laugh. Then she does. Sarah and I laugh, too.

My thoughts and feelings, for once, are exactly right.

"Let's catch some wind!" Flossie punches the air.

I walk to the front of the boat and move the wheel hand over hand, turning us west.

Back to the Key Peninsula and Grandma. Bringing Flossie and me, and Sarah, too, toward peace and safety.

Our own little *happily ever after* at last.

The End

***

Please share your honest review of *The Octopus Under the Bridge* on Amazon!

***

Writing a review means YOUR ideas get published online! Reviews help other kids decide whether or not to read the book. They also help me become a better writer, and think about whether to write a sequel. I read every single review I get, and it makes my day to get a review from a young reader. Remember to get parent permission before posting online. Thank you!

Love,
Alice

P.S. Sail over to my Alice Kinerk author page on Facebook, or find me @alice_kinerk on Instagram and Twitter. Or check out alicekinerk.com to read about the anarchist history that inspired this story, learn about the Giant Pacific Octopus, and the Tacoma Narrows Bridge, find out how I became a writer, contact me, and more. I love hearing from readers!

Made in the USA
Middletown, DE
16 August 2020